Before Wings

Beth Goobie is an award-winning children's author whose novels have won and been shortlisted for the most prestigious prizes in her native Canada, including the Governor General's Award for Children's Literature and the Canadian Library Association Young Adult Book of the Year Award. She graduated with an English degree and has worked with abused children for many years. *The Lottery* was shortlisted for the Ottaker's Children's Book Prize.

'Beth Goobie just might be the best YA writer in the country. She is, certainly, the most intense, most poetic. And *Before Wings* is, to my mind, her finest book to date. It is *sensationful*. The words glow and crackle like summer lightning, vivid and fervent. Again and again she strikes you down with a turn of phrase, and yet, miraculously, the writing never gets in the way of the story, which has the pulse-quickening pace of a thriller. *Before Wings* is many things: a love story, a mystery, a heartfelt prayer, but, best of all, it is a marvellous good read.' Tim Wynne-Jones

Before Wings

Beth Goobie

faber and faber

First published in Canada and the USA in 2000
by Orca Book Publishers
Box 5626, Station B, Victoria, BC,
v8r 6s4, Canada

First published in the UK by
Faber and Faber Limited in 2008
3 Queen Square London wc1n 3au

Typeset by Faber and Faber Limited
Printed in England by CPI Bookmarque, Croydon cro 4td

A CIP record for this book
is available from the British Library

The author gratefully acknowledges the Saskatchewan Arts Board
and Canada Council grants that funded the writing of this book

isbn 978–0–571–23351–9

2 4 6 8 10 9 7 5 3 1

Before Wings

Part I

One

The spirits had brought a cold, grey day. Adrien watched them hover above the lake, curling in and out of themselves with the wind. Female and young, they were sending their breath across the water in mournful blasts, kicking up whitecaps, dashing spray on the rocks, calling up storms. These spirits still wanted to kick ass even though they were long dead. Adrien gave them a grim thumbs-up and they wailed in return, their bodies twisting into the shrill notes of their voices. She could almost make out words, the same phrase called over and over, their smoky-coloured bodies shifting with each syllable.

'You'll get soaked.' A maternal yank hauled Adrien back from the water's edge as a large wave came in with a crash. 'Geezzzus,' hissed her mother, pulling her soaked sweatshirt out from herself. 'C'mon, let's get you into dry clothes before you see us off.'

'Mom,' wailed Adrien, 'I'm fifteen!'

'All daydreamers are two years old while they're dreaming.' Her mother turned to follow the path that led up from the beach, stepping into the sudden lift of insect wings.

'Ugh,' yelped Adrien, flapping at the bugs. They were everywhere, flitting through the camp-grounds and along the beach, piles of their pale bodies rotting on the sand. The zillions that were still alive rose in a swarm of translucent wings with every step she took, settling all over her. When she pulled them off, there was a slight suction that made her think of leeches, and she waved her arms wildly as she followed her mother up the steep ridge and away from the beach. Ahead stretched a wide grassy area that led to the dining hall, office and parking lot. A potential bug lurked on every blade of grass. As Adrien and her mother crossed the lawn, the ground was a continual explosion of silent wings, the air filled with flight.

'What were you watching?' her mother asked casually.

Ever since Adrien could remember, her mother had been casually trying to get inside her head. Her mother loved her very, very much. Too much. Adrien felt that love closing in and fought on dim, short wings to fly free. 'Just the weather.'

'Just the outer galaxies?'

'Something closer.'

Outside the office, her father leaned against the car, talking to his sister. As Adrien approached, his voice called out with a forced cheeriness. 'Fell into the lake already, I see. And took your mother for a swim.'

'Got an extra sweatshirt, Erin?' asked Adrien's mother.

'Will I get it back?' Aunt Erin demanded.

'Would I want to keep it?' replied Adrien's mother. She dressed urban; Aunt Erin dressed second-hand rural. Still quibbling, the two women headed for the master cabin where Aunt Erin slept, plotting the next day's camp schedule in her dreams.

Adrien's father rumpled her hair. 'Water's wet today, huh?'

'Yeah, wet.'

'You're carrying a few travellers.' He picked several bugs off her shoulders. Glancing down, Adrien saw she was covered.

'Yuck! What're these things?' She swiped at them, but the bugs had to be pulled off one by one. Released, they fluttered a short distance and sank into the grass.

'Mayflies,' said her father.

'Mayflies? But it's late June.'

'Americans get them in May, so that's what they're called. Warm weather comes later to us frozen, ice-bound Canadian Prairie types, and so do bugs. Don't worry. Mayflies last a couple of weeks and then they're gone.'

'You mean I'm going to have to wear bugs for two weeks?'

'Then the mosquitoes hit full force,' said her father, a smile floating over his serious tone. 'You sure you want to stay here all summer? Your aunt's an iron woman. I wouldn't want her for my boss. Older sister was bad enough.'

Adrien shrugged. 'I can always come home.'

Her father winced at her lack of enthusiasm. She sneezed and he took off his red lumber jacket, wrapping it around her. 'Last thing we need is you getting sick on your first day.'

'So I come home in a coffin,' Adrien muttered softly, but her father caught it. A whiplash of pain crossed his face and she regretted saying it, knew he would replay the moment endlessly, trying to figure out what he could have said to inspire her, change her, turn her life around.

'I'll be fine, Dad.' She leaned into him and he hugged her tightly. This one brief moment was something she could give him, solid in the warm circle of his arms while the wind moaned through the overhead spruce and spirits wailed across the lake.

'I know you will,' he said into her hair.

They waited in silence until Adrien's mother returned, wearing a thin, ratty Camp Lakeshore sweat-shirt with multiple paint stains and a ripped elbow.

'I want that back,' Aunt Erin insisted, following her.

'I'm comfortable in it.'

'I bet you've been wearing this since the Tories were wiped out.'

'Longer. Since we repatriated the Constitution.'

The adults laughed. There were hugs all around, and penetrating, teary looks from her mother.

'Keep the jacket,' said her father.

'It's too big, Dad.'

'Keep it anyway,' he said, patting her shoulder. Then they were in the car, her father reversing, tooting the horn while her mother waved furiously. Adrien listened to the sound of tyres on gravel as the car disappeared around the bend. Every ten seconds, her father tooted the horn as the car made its way along the road that wound through the large wooded area surrounding the camp. It was a long road; they were holding onto her as long as they could. Finally, he sent out a chipper series of toots to let her know they had reached the gate and were passing through. Letting go. Gone.

The wind blew a dark song through the lift and fall of trees. The huge air was sharp-edged with the scent of spruce. Adrien turned to look at the lake. From here the spirits were indistinguishable, part of the bruised grey of water and sky.

'I hate these,' she complained, pulling a mayfly off her arm.

'Don't bite,' said her aunt. 'Die off the first week of July.'

Adrien shot her a quick glance.

'You'll catch your death in those wet clothes.' Aunt Erin's pale blue eyes didn't blink. She had said the word and wasn't fumbling to take it back, cover it over, apologize. Maybe she had intended it. 'Hot chocolate?'

'I'm dying for some.' Adrien twisted the word, drawing it out.

'Bull,' Aunt Erin said shortly, and turned towards the kitchen.

Adrien took the thick white mug of hot chocolate and headed to the staff cabins to change into dry clothes.

Though it had been Aunt Erin's suggestion, she was relieved to escape extended conversation. There was something about her aunt – thick, gnarled and pale – that reminded Adrien of a Group of Seven painting. The one with the glacier. Or maybe the tree stump. It wasn't her aunt's face or the way she looked, it was the way she stood within trees, sky and wind. Aunt Erin sure fitted into this place. Her first Camp Lakeshore job had been as a counsellor when she was eighteen, and now she ran the camp. She had never married – Erin Wood made no place for small intimacies. Just looking at her, Adrien could tell her heart was a shoreline vast with water and sky, shifting shale and driftwood. Not a human in sight. Iron woman, like her father said.

The cabin smelled of wood and disinfectant. Someone had opened the windows and cleaned the rooms in preparation for staff training. In two days, Camp Lakeshore would be invaded by teenagers and university students, hired as counsellors, skills instructors and maintenance crew. Adrien would be working in the Tuck-'n'-Tack shop at minimum wage, selling candy and T-shirts. The alternative was spending the summer in Saskatoon, watching her father water the lawn while her mother propped up her tomato plants, and all three of them waited for the Big One to hit. Any time Adrien made a sudden movement, her parents would turn towards her, fear widening their eyes. Sometimes her mother moaned out loud.

Aunt Erin wouldn't follow her around like a worried sheep. She had made Adrien hot chocolate, then booted her out, saying she had things to do. 'Sunday afternoon, grounds are quiet. Go out and explore. Supper's at five.'

The cabin echoed Adrien's footsteps. Small shuffling sounds crept along the walls. Birch and spruce crowded the windows, casting the room in a deep green light that shifted with the wind. She changed into a dry sweatsuit and a T-shirt, and draped her wet clothes over the other bed. The cabin had four bedrooms, each with two beds. She would have a roommate, someone else filling this quiet green space with loud talk and movement, conversation and judgment. Quickly, Adrien pulled on her father's lumber jacket and left the cabin.

She headed through the wooded area enclosing the staff cabins, then out onto the wide expanse of lawn with its frantic mayflies, towards the lake. A path led down a steep ridge to the beach. To her left was the dock, in front and to the right extended the yellow rope and buoys that marked the swimming area. Adrien climbed the lifeguard's chair and sat staring out. The spirits had gone down into the water and she could barely make them out – shadows that rose and sank with the swelling waves. Abruptly the sun emerged and painted the landscape with startling blues, browns and greens. Overhead, the shrill cries of gulls wheeled through brilliant clouds.

Her aneurysm had exploded out of a moment like this, a moment without expectations, a moment like any other. A similar sky had stretched without interruption into forever, the earth had run ahead of her feet, sure of itself, no widening cracks, no earthquakes,

9

no tricks. Sure, there had been the headache, building for days, but who paid attention to headaches, even bad ones? They weren't as real as the grins of her friends, snapping their gum and making wisecracks as she stepped up to bat, the gym teacher winding up for the pitch. She had reached it, had fought the massive pain in her head for that hit, could still remember the exact, contained explosion as bat met ball, the sweet ache travelling her arms. The ball had soared into the blue like a heart, leaving her below within dizziness, pain and nausea. Still fighting, she had managed to take two steps, headed towards first base.

The second explosion had gone off inside her head, tiny sharp lights that swelled in a dizzying wave. There had been a sound to it, a thousand voices calling in one long note from some faraway place, and for a moment she had thought the light in her head was a bright hand reaching into her brain to scoop her up and take her home. Then the sensation of falling had taken over – falling into herself, arms and legs collapsing, bones and muscles meaning nothing as her face came down hard in the dirt.

She had been gone by the time she had eaten that dirt, had no memory of her friends screaming, the gym teacher fending off their curiosity, the girl who had run to the office. Or the ambulance that had rammed itself over the kerb and torn across the field to where she lay unconscious, having vomited and shit her pants. No one had told her any of this: she had reconstructed it from overheard conversations and some reading she had done on brain aneurysms once she had been let out of bed. That hadn't been for months, and then there had been rehab and home schooling. Much of it she had been too stupid, too dozed out, to remember. Once she had got back enough of her brain, there wasn't much she wanted to recall. She was a year behind in school. Her friends had moved on, probably confusing her with someone who had died in a TV special. It had taken her months to regain basic motor skills. Sometimes her brain would still backfire and her legs give out; she would be eating dirt again. It was difficult to trust a body that had betrayed her so completely. Even now, she sat waiting for the one essential neuron to misfire, and her brain to go up in that final apocalyptic explosion of light. Rising, she would hear a thousand voices calling her to the faraway. *Dying, this is dying, wings of light, lifting upward out of* –

A rock flew by on her right and skipped twice before sinking. Startled, Adrien turned to see a dark-haired boy her own age sitting on the ridge, hunched in a blue lumber jacket and covered in a smattering of mayflies. Her eyes narrowed, but he didn't glance at her, so she turned back to the lake without speaking. Another rock flew by, and another.

'You're Erin's kid?' he asked finally.

'I'm not her kid.'

'You look just like her.'

Everyone said this. It was ridiculous. Adrien's eyes were hazel, her hair a long, frizzy blonde-brown. Her aunt's hair was wheat blonde, straight and cut like a boy's.

'Yeah, like a truck looks like a Honda,' she snapped.

'Which one are you, the truck or the Honda?'

'I'm the one with the flat tyres.'

The boy's eyebrows lifted, then his face lapsed into moodiness and he threw more rocks. Adrien watched them soar and drop into the water. Down, down – she was being pulled down with the rocks, the day darkening, the air growing thick. Bubbles left her mouth, rising to where other people breathed, effortless and free.

'You're dying,' said the boy.

It took a moment to clear the water from her brain. When she turned, the ridge was empty, the tall line of grass along its edge bending before the wind.

'There was a boy hanging around the lake this afternoon.'

The large room rounded and deepened Adrien's voice. Perched on a stool, she watched Aunt Erin make supper for two in a kitchen designed to feed hundreds. She supposed, she thought slowly, her aunt was pretty. She had the kind of face that drew eyes, but it was remote and alone like a profile carved into a rock cliff. Aunt Erin spoke to people out of necessity, and then she was done with them.

'That'd be Paul Marchand,' Aunt Erin said crisply. 'Lives near here. Does maintenance for me.'

'He's weird.'

Aunt Erin gave her a pale blue look. 'Got a sixth sense. It's a burden and don't you forget it. Carries it well.'

Adrien pushed out the words in raw, heavy chunks. 'He told me I was dying.'

Aunt Erin stopped moving and stood with her head down. 'Well, and isn't that what you're always telling people?' she said finally and reached for the salt.

Adrien flushed, her heart jerking unsteadily. 'But I didn't tell him.'

Aunt Erin pushed through another slight pause. 'Probably picked up on your thoughts. The boy reads minds. Hardly have to speak to him some days, just knows what I want done. How many cobs of corn?' She lifted the lid off a pot of boiling water.

Without answering, Adrien pushed back her stool and went over to a window. Her heart was a dark door, slamming in the wind. She put out a finger to trace the coolness of the glass and felt nothing. Outside, rain fell steadily. 'D'you think he's right?'

Aunt Erin closed the pot lid with a clank. 'Like I said, picking up on your thoughts. Walk around in a storm cloud like you do, you broadcast loud and clear. Hamburgers are ready.'

'I'm not hungry.'

'Suit yourself.' Aunt Erin pulled a stool to the main counter and began to eat in silence. Gradually, very gradually, Adrien's heart slowed. Rain slid every which way down the other side of the glass, collected in small pools.

'I think he's weird,' she said emphatically. 'I'm not talking to him.'

'Don't have to talk to anyone you don't want.'

Adrien sat down and picked up a hamburger. 'I like cheeseburgers.'

'Cheese is in the fridge.'

Her mother would have asked if she wanted cheese. Sighing heavily, Adrien took a bite and began to chew.

The rain continued. After cleaning up, Aunt Erin asked if she wanted to walk to the corrals to see the horses, but Adrien headed for her cabin. She hadn't realized she was tired, but when she made her bed and lay down, exhaustion poured through her. There was something about the huge, windy, spruce-scented air of this place. At home, her parents maintained a cheerful static, quickly covering her comments about death and doom as if her words were blood – when she made a wise-crack about dying, she began haemorrhaging and they had to staunch the flow, shut her up. *Shut her up*. Sometimes she screamed, 'I could die, you know. I could die' – anything to cut through the loving crap. Silenced, her parents would stare helplessly. Once she had yelled, 'Why don't you have another kid, just fucking conceive!' Her mother's face had crumpled, her father had gone white, but they hadn't said what they were thinking: *We want to give you all our love until you're gone.*

It was Aunt Erin who had suggested Adrien work at Camp Lakeshore for the summer. She had called her niece directly and invited her. 'Can't pay you much, won't be a millionaire. Just working in the store, nothing too strenuous.'

A few hours and it had been strenuous all right. Some weird boy telling her she was dying. Aunt Erin treating her like a mental deficient. The wind moaning in the trees, opening up places in the air, calling spirits.

Since her aneurysm, Adrien had been able to see spirits. Perhaps her brain circuitry had altered, or the worlds had rearranged themselves to give her a taste of the afterlife. She didn't see them constantly, but there was often a hint of something smudging the corner of a room, shifting behind a tree, or wailing across a lake. This didn't frighten her, just made it difficult to focus on the here and now. It was like being pulled simultaneously in different directions. She was standing in a shadow land between two worlds and being asked to choose, but didn't know how to take those first steps towards the humans reaching out to her, their voices calling, 'Come, come.' Their smiles were too vivid. She kept fending them off.

Aunt Erin and the weird boy didn't play the game of life, pretending there was hope. Paul Marchand was right. She was dying. Maybe not at this very moment, but it would come. The blood vessels in her brain were weaker since the aneurysm – they could tear at any moment, rip the life out of her. Her body would drop, her spirit rise . . . to do what? Float endlessly in a grey smudge through rooms, watching the living go on without her? Join that line of spirits howling across the lake? What was it they had been calling, over and over?

Adrien slipped on a raincoat and made her way towards the water, looking down to keep the wind out of her face. The mayflies had been grounded by the rain, and a cold aloneness spread out on all sides. Why had she come to this place? she wondered miserably. A place where no one knew her, no one loved her. She was an aneurysm victim. Didn't Aunt Erin know she had to be careful not to get upset, not to exert herself and stress her blood vessels? Reaching the ridge, she was about to follow the path down to the shore when she saw her aunt standing motionless on the beach, hood down, her yellow jacket flapping in the wind. Out on the lake, the spirits moved in a restless line, a grey glow that was easy to distinguish in the dark – the vague shapes of five girls moving in and out of themselves, grieving like smoke.

Aunt Erin was watching them. Unaware of her niece, she stood staring directly at the spirits. There was no doubt about it, they were as clear to her as they were to Adrien.

Abruptly she turned and came up the path. Startled, Adrien stepped back. As her aunt peaked the ridge, she looked straight at Adrien, her face split wide with sorrow. Without speaking she passed by, walking across the lawn towards the dining hall while Adrien stared after her, tasting her aunt's loneliness, a heavy salt in her throat.

Two

She slept heavily, through dreams of heaving water and a night sky coiled with clouds. Formless voices called through slow chaos. When she woke, she was sweating, her scalp soaked, even though the cabin held an early morning coolness. The rain had stopped.

It took a few minutes to place the unfamiliar bed, the rough blankets, the pillow that smelled of closed-in places. About her the room danced with a rustling emerald light, and for a brief moment she was sure she had stepped through to one of her dreams, waking in another life where she could be free of wondering if something was always about to tear open inside her head.

The snapping of branches brought her bolt upright. Suddenly Adrien realized she was alone in a cabin, and something was moving against the outer wall. Wrapping a blanket around herself, she crept to the window, but saw only the lift and toss of easy green trees. More sounds came from the opposite side of the cabin. Heart thudding, she slunk down the narrow hall and peeked into an empty bedroom. A shadow fell across the window, and then abruptly a face peered in.

'Close the window and I'll take out the screen,' Paul said. 'I'm washing windows.'

'I was *sleeping*,' complained Adrien.

'Close the window,' he repeated, holding up a squeegee.

'Close your own window.' She turned to leave.

'I'll have to come in.'

'Go and do another cabin first.'

'This is the last one.'

'So wait *five* minutes while I get dressed. What time is it, anyway?'

'Eight-thirty.'

'Most people start work at nine.'

He retreated and she decided she had won. But what if he sneaked around the cabin, she thought in alarm, and watched through the window while she dressed? Or came inside? Locking the bedroom door, she pulled down the blind before changing into jeans and a T-shirt. Then she washed her face, brushed her teeth, and carefully combed her hair. Make the prophet of doom wait, she thought with satisfaction. When she finally emerged from the cabin, she found Paul sitting on the front steps, smoking. As she stepped off the side of the small square porch into a flurry of mayflies, he turned to look at her, his face expressionless as yesterday, except for his eyes.

'What?' she snapped, flushing.

He shrugged.

'Isn't it against the rules to smoke at Camp Lakeshore?'

He shrugged again.

She hesitated. 'So can I have one?'

He gave just the hint of a smile as he pulled a pack from his shirt pocket and tossed it to her. She missed and had to bend to pick it up. So what, she thought. She couldn't be expected to be an athlete these days. A yellow lighter was tucked into the left side. Lighting up, she inhaled deeply. This was one thing she hadn't fully con-sidered when she had agreed to come for the summer, but then she hadn't known about the no-smoking rule until Aunt Erin had sent the long list of *Rules for Staff,* one week after the phone call. Not that it mattered on an official level – she was underage and Aunt Erin was hardly likely to sell them to her at the Tuck-'n'-Tack store – but it had meant that none of the other staff members would be carrying any for an easy bum. After thinking through all the ways she could get caught smuggling in a carton, Adrien had decided this would be the perfect opportunity to quit. Perfect as in no two ways about it.

'Thanks.' She started picking mayflies off her T-shirt.

He returned the pack to his pocket. 'Any time, Angel.'

'My name's Adrien.'

He looked directly at her. 'I know.'

The opportunity was wide open. She had been pok-ing and prodding people for two years, looking for this moment, and here it was. She gulped air, then said slowly, 'How come you said I was dying?'

His eyes didn't leave her face. 'Aren't we all?'

She dragged on her cigarette. 'Yeah, but I *am*. Did my aunt tell you?'

He dropped his stub and ground it out, then slid it under the porch. 'Erin doesn't talk about people. She's good that way.'

'So how'd you know?'

He linked his hands behind his head and stretched, cracking bones all over his body. 'I've dreamt my own death a hundred different times. A hundred different ways. It never quite gets me; I always wake up just before.' His eyes narrowed and he stared off moodily. 'It's always the same day, the same place, but each time it happens a different way.'

'They can't all be right,' said Adrien.

'No,' Paul agreed. 'But why always the same time and place? I figure I choose the way it gets me, that's all.'

She forced a laugh. 'You're nuts.'

'Then why d'you ask me?'

They watched each other in the quiet morning air.

'You still haven't told me how you knew I was dying,' Adrien managed finally.

'Just a feeling.' He picked up a bucket and turned to go.

'Hey,' she called after him. 'Can you tell when it's going to happen . . . to me?'

He looked back at her. 'It's not clear.'

'So when's your big date?'

'Want to watch?'

'Just wondering.'

His face intensified. 'You'll be there. I've seen it. Hide the butt, eh?' A silvery swarm of bugs rose as he pushed into the bush at the back of the cabin. She listened to the squeegee swish in the bucket and drip as it rose. Paul swore.

She took one last drag at her cigarette, ground out the butt, and slid it under the porch.

'Hey, Angel,' called Paul. 'Would you *please* go inside and close the windows?'

Her lips twitched with the hint of a smile. Surrounded by sunlit bug wings, she followed the path through the trees towards the dining hall for breakfast.

Three women in polyester uniforms stood at the kitchen's main counter, opening large boxes of canned food. Their voices could be heard from the dining hall's main entrance, interrupting one another and breaking into volleys of laughter. In the erratic torrent of words, Adrien couldn't hear a single syllable of English. Cautiously she peered into the kitchen. Camp Lakeshore's cooking staff didn't look like aliens, just three middle-aged women, bulging at the sides and wearing orthopaedic shoes. Hairnets and weird words.

One woman saw her and broke into heavily accented English. 'You're Adrien, right?'

Adrien smiled with relief.

'Such a pretty girl,' said the woman. 'Looks just like Erin, eh?'

The hairnets nodded enthusiastically.

'Um, could I have breakfast?' Adrien asked.

'Breakfast?' The first woman rolled her eyes dramatically. 'Maybe you could show up before noon?'

'Just bread and water?' Adrien hedged.

The women whooped. Corn Flakes, milk and bread appeared and she ate, listening as they lapsed into their weird language. Why didn't they speak English if they understood it? she wondered. Casually she tried to guess what they were talking about. The old country? Their children? Husbands? Sex? At the last thought, Adrien almost laughed out loud. Maybe they were discussing their latest pap smear tests. Cancer – did the hairnets ever think about death? From their whoops, giggles and snorts, it didn't sound like it. As Adrien scooped up her last spoonful of cereal, the first woman smiled at her. 'Just leave your dishes in the sink,' she said, returning to English. 'We'll get them later.'

'Um,' Adrien asked hesitantly, 'where do you come from?'

The women gave each other sly smiles.

'Ah, she wants us to go back to where we come from,' said one.

'Wants our jobs,' said another. 'Wants to work on her varicose veins.'

'It's these lovely uniforms and hairnets,' said the third. 'Everyone wants to wear them.'

'Tsk tsk tsk,' said the first. 'Finish your school, then think about stealing our jobs.'

Leaving her bowl where it sat, Adrien fled the kitchen, out into the trees where she stood, her cheeks burning. *Old hags*, she thought furiously. She didn't want their lousy jobs. For all she cared, they could cook pork and sausages in every lousy camp in the entire country. *Rude* – they were *rude*. Turning this way and that, Adrien kicked at tree roots and flailed at mayflies until her face cooled. God, did she need a cigarette. That's what she should do, she thought suddenly – learn how to ask for a cigarette in whatever gibberish those hags were speaking, and run *that* by them. She would show them. By the end of summer, she would be fluent in asking for drugs, needles, condoms and porn in *their* language. Every morning she would come up with something different. For example: *Excuse me, but do you have the latest issue of* Playgirl? *I lent mine to the campers and they won't give it back.*

She arrived at the office to find Aunt Erin already there. 'Great,' said her aunt, looking up from her desk. 'Today, you'll do inventory for the store. Count stuff.' She grinned as she spoke, but she looked tired, her eyes puffy. Briefly, the memory of last night's scene at the lake passed between them, a shadow of cold wind and rain. Frowning, Aunt Erin pressed the bridge of her nose, pushing at something in her head. Pushing it away. 'Leave the mayflies outside,' she said.

Adrien stepped out onto the porch. All over her body the bugs sat in a resting position, their wings folded together and pointed upwards. They didn't struggle as she pulled them off, but there was always a slight suction, as if their little buggy feet were holding

23

on for dear life. *Yuck*, she thought, watching each one flutter away. *Putrid. Barbaric. Go thou to thy doom.*

As she came back inside, a lawnmower started up. 'On grass already,' Aunt Erin said. 'Boy's fast as ever.'

On the other side of the room, boxes labelled 'T-shirts Medium', 'Sweatshirts Large' and 'Buttons' were stacked along the wall. Adrien was more interested in the ones marked 'Coffee Crisp' and 'Smarties'.

'No eating the merchandise,' Aunt Erin admonished, following her gaze. 'I'll show you what to do.'

'I can count,' said Adrien.

'There's last summer's records, and records from over the winter,' said Aunt Erin, ignoring her. 'Schools come out for the day. Religious groups and conferences rent the place. Need to make sure everything's in order. Glad you're here to do it.'

Getting to her feet, she pointed to a storage room at the back of the office where boxes were stacked half-way to the ceiling. 'Hope you like counting,' she quipped, then led Adrien outside and around the building to where an awning opened out of the north wall. During the summer months, Tuck-'n'-Tack operated like a concession booth. Briskly Aunt Erin handed Adrien the ring of keys that unlocked the door, the cabinets and the large service window. 'Lots of air conditioning,' she said. 'Here's the lever that lowers the awning.'

She demonstrated and Adrien played with it, watching the blue-and-white striped canvas yawn outward, then shrink back in. *Out, in, out, in.*

'Easily entertained,' observed her aunt. 'Good to see.'

Before Adrien could protest, she continued, 'When you're working in Tuck-'n'-Tack, kids'll come by with their counsellors. Every cabin's got its daily time slot.' She made Adrien practise unlocking and locking everything, then showed her where to hang the key ring on the office wall. 'How many summers were you here?' she asked vaguely.

'Five,' said Adrien. She had been booked for a sixth, but her brain had blown that June.

'Here's the books,' said her aunt, handing Adrien several ledgers and ignoring yet another obvious opportunity for sympathy. Quickly she explained how to decipher the numbers and columns, then returned to her desk. One by one, Adrien began to open the boxes in front of her. There were *zillions* of T-shirts and sweatshirts, each with two sailing boats and five tiny waves.

'These are ugly colours,' she said.

'What?' Aunt Erin looked up from her desk.

'Kids don't like these colours,' said Adrien.

'Blue, green and red?'

'They're all dark,' explained Adrien. 'You need neon. Lime green, laser lemon and hot pink. A bright blue. You'd sell a lot more.'

'Thanks for the suggestion.' Aunt Erin returned to her paperwork.

Heat slapped itself across Adrien's face. Staring at her aunt's bent head, she said slowly, 'Don't talk to me like that. I'm not slave labour.'

'That's right. You can go home if you want.' Aunt Erin didn't lift her head.

'Well, maybe I will.'

'Phone's right here. Help yourself.'

Silence pulsed between them.

'Why don't you like me?' Adrien asked in a small voice.

Aunt Erin sat very still, her head down. 'Like has nothing to do with it,' she said. 'You're working at a job for pay. I tell you what to do and you do it. Don't order your boss around. May as well learn that from me, or it'll get harder for you later.'

What later? Adrien almost asked, but the phone rang and Aunt Erin picked it up. 'Camp Lakeshore,' she said calmly, looking out of the window.

Footsteps crossed the office porch, and Paul peered through the screen door. 'Coffee break. Coming?'

Adrien knew he meant smoke break and started to get up, but Aunt Erin covered the phone and said, 'Just started. Give it another hour. Then you get ten minutes.' She returned to the phone.

Paul's eyebrows floated upwards. 'I'll come back in an hour,' he said and left.

After the phone call, Aunt Erin left the office without speaking. Rigid, Adrien sat staring at the box of medium-size navy-blue T-shirts she was counting. They were more than ugly, she thought stubbornly, they were archaic. Camp Lakeshore's logo hadn't changed in over a decade, and the two toy sailing boats and five dinky waves looked like something out of a kid's colouring book. Didn't Aunt Erin know she was competing with extraterrestrials and Marilyn Manson?

Getting up, she wandered around the office. It held the usual boring stuff: memo pads, staplers, a calendar with scenic trees, copies of summer scheduling. There were two wall clocks, one on the east wall and one on the west, catching the sun as it came up and went down. Aunt Erin had everything clocked, organized and filed into place – except, Adrien thought grimly, her niece-from-the-city, and *she* wasn't going to fit into her aunt's neat schemes without a fight. Maybe she would just have her final aneurysm here and now, throw up and die all over her aunt's tidy desk. Wouldn't that throw a wrench into things? She could just imagine Aunt Erin discovering the body, checking for a pulse, then calling Mom and Dad. There would be tears, profuse apologies. Meticulously Adrien explored every possible angle of 'I was such a lousy aunt, I killed her with my terrible attitude'. It gave immense satisfaction for several minutes, then waned.

Idly she fingered through a stack of papers on her aunt's desk. As she did, her hand shifted the mat beneath them, uncovering the corner of a small photograph. Curious, she slid out the picture and scanned it. A group of girls her own age looked back at her, grinning at the camera. They were all in swimsuits, as was their counsellor, a young woman with wheat-blonde hair and pale blue eyes – Aunt Erin in a Speedo, holding a life-jacket and grinning as if she hadn't a care in the world. Stunned, Adrien couldn't believe how much they looked alike. There on Aunt Erin's face she saw her own forehead, nose and mouth, ridged cheekbones and jutting chin. Two of the girls had draped adoring arms around her neck. Two more had wrapped their arms around her waist. They must, thought Adrien drily, have been nuts.

She slipped the photograph into her wallet. There was a lot of information in this picture and she wanted to study it. Later, she would return it. Maybe. *If* her aunt behaved herself and started treating her with respect. Comforting herself with a Coffee Crisp, Adrien went back to counting last year's ugly unsold T-shirts.

In exactly one hour she was sitting on the porch steps, waiting for her cigarette. Aunt Erin was nowhere in sight and she had counted so many T-shirts that a myriad ugly sailing boats were floating through the dazzling waters of her brain. In the distance, she heard the sound of a mower cut off, then approaching footsteps. Frantic mayflies exploded in every direction, and Paul came into view.

'C'mon,' he said. 'I know a place.' As the morning had grown warm, he had chucked the lumber jacket. Already his tanned face was darker.

'I'm *dying* for one.'

He gave a slow, appreciative smile. 'You didn't bring any?'

'I read the rules.'

'Yeah, I'm glad I don't live on the grounds.'

He turned onto a path that disappeared into a shimmering dance of leaves and bug wings. Swearing, Adrien waved wildly around her head. 'I wouldn't do this for any other reason, y'know.'

He turned and grinned back at her. 'No?'

She rolled her eyes and looked away. This was the way she handled boys at school: smoked their cigarettes and sidestepped their comments and hands. When she was alone, she thought about the possibilities – thought about them a lot – but she never let them happen. There was something about touching, coming that close – she was sure all that heat would light up her brain like a Molotov cocktail.

'Erin not around?' asked Paul as they continued along the path.

'We had a fight and she took off.'

'Already?' He ducked through two spruce trees and she followed, emerging into a small clearing. *More mayflies*, thought Adrien. A halo of wings had settled onto Paul's hair and shoulders. 'This is where they teach schoolkids to build lean-tos,' he said.

'We're going to build one and crawl in to smoke?' asked Adrien.

He grinned again, scanning her face. Adrien rolled her eyes emphatically, realizing how she had set herself up. 'Give me a smoke,' she said, delicately picking wings off her shirt front. *Fluttering on her breast. How embarrassing.*

He pulled out the pack. 'So what did you fight about?'

Impatient, she shrugged. 'I just told her she needed to sell T-shirts in better colours. She bit off my head.'

He handed her a cigarette. 'Doesn't sound like her.'

'Yeah, well, I don't like her much.'

'Why?' He lit her cigarette, then his own.

'She's bossy.'

'She's the boss.'

'I don't like being bossed.' Adrien wandered to the edge of the clearing, watching bugs rise through shafts of sun that cut through the trees. *How could air colour itself like that?* she wondered. *Green shadows and gold streams of light. Even the bugs looked pretty out here.* Pulling one off her throat, she watched it flutter off.

'Tough city girl,' said Paul.

She turned to find him assessing her, his eyes travelling slowly. 'Stop that,' she said, waving her hand and breaking his gaze so he turned to look into the woods. 'I'm not easy, if that's what you mean.'

'No, Angel, nothing about you is easy.'

'Stop calling me Angel. You want me to call you –' She searched for an appropriate name. '– Darth Vader?'

Unexpectedly, he laughed. 'Darth Vader and Angel – that'd make a great team. Cover all the angles.'

'Do you always think about death?'

'Do you?'

She paused, considering. 'The possibility is always lurking.'

'Isn't it for everyone?'

'Not like me.'

'That makes two of us, eh?'

This time she assessed him, the broad face, thick eyebrows, wide mouth. His nose beaked slightly, and his hair was shaggy, down to his collar. Lower than that she was not

30

going to look now, but just wait until his back was turned.

'How old are you?' she asked.

'Sixteen this July. You?'

'November. So how d'you get your smokes?'

'There's always someone who'll sell to minors.'

'Yeah,' she agreed. No matter how many signs were posted, teenagers found out who was open for business. 'You do anything else?'

'Drugs?' He shot her a look. 'I've got enough shit happening in my head. You?'

'Someone spiked my pop at school once, but I've never done anything on my own.'

'You want to?'

'It was too weird.' Even the memory of the event gave her the willies – the sudden lights happening in her head, crawling into a bathroom corner to sweat it out. After that, she had never shared another can of pop. 'What d'you think happens,' she asked abruptly, 'y'know, when you die?'

'Pain,' he said softly.

'Yeah, but I mean is there overwhelming darkness or do you go to a place of light?'

'I don't know,' he shrugged. 'I never get to the actual moment of dying. All I see is another way it's gonna happen, coming straight at me.'

'I think it's light,' she said firmly. 'That's how it was for me the first time. I had a brain aneurysm two years ago. My whole head exploded with light.'

'So what was it like?' asked Paul. 'Meeting God?'

She shook her head. 'It wasn't God. More like a star

31

dying in my brain. Y'know how they explode when they go out? It was like that – a huge explosion, nuclear bomb, the end of the world. Boom!' She snapped her fingers. 'Lots of people walk around with a blood vessel bulging in their brain and they don't even know it. Sometimes you don't feel any symptoms. It just ruptures, and you drop dead.'

He stood quietly on the other side of the clearing. 'So that's the way it'll be for you, eh?'

She took a quick breath. 'Yeah.'

'At least you know how you're going,' he said.

Three

Late morning, the sky clouded over. Sharp gusts of wind kept slamming the office screen door. Two core staff who worked year-round at the camp returned from a day off and stood bantering with Aunt Erin on the porch as if they actually enjoyed her company. Suspicious, Adrien watched for any signs of suck-up or kiss-ass, but there didn't seem to be any. *Brain slumming*, she eventually decided. In order to survive — no, *like* — her aunt's tyrannical leadership, they had tossed mental efficiency out of the window and reduced their brains to low gear. Well, that didn't mean she had to. At noon, she recorded her current total of small, ugly red sweatshirts, got to her feet, and said. 'I'm going for lunch.'

'Be back at one,' Aunt Erin replied.

As if Adrien couldn't figure that out. Banging the screen door, she ran heavily down the steps, then stood letting the wind hit her full in the face. From here she could see clear across the freshly cut lawn to the lake, which rolled and heaved under an approaching storm. Thunder rumbled faintly in a slate-grey sky. Low to the

33

water flickered an eerie fork of lightning, and a small shiver of white echoed through the inside of Adrien's head. Again, lightning forked the entire horizon, and Adrien stared, fascinated. It was like watching her own brain, the knife-lines of electricity that sliced through its heavy mass. Calling, the sky was calling her into the grey pulp of its brain, the dazzle of its forked currents. *Come, we know you, come and be with us.*

Several members of staff could be seen heading towards the dining hall. Someone shouted her name, but instead of responding Adrien turned and ran across a lawn of translucent wings towards a sky that broke open, again and again, into fierce light. Reaching the ridge, she started down the path, and saw the spirits darting over the water's surface like dragonflies. She could make out arms and legs, different hair lengths, even breasts, but their faces were shadowed. And the spirits were moaning, a low sound that seemed to be calling the storm towards the beach where Adrien had come to a halt and stood pushing to stay erect in the wind. As she listened, she became certain the spirits were calling something specific: a short phrase, several words, repeated like the lightning that snaked the sky. Another sheer burst of white tore through the clouds and Adrien stepped forward into the wild lake, the call of the spirit girls, the energy of their brains dying across sky. Into some understood sameness.

'Are you crazy?' a voice shouted behind her.

Someone grabbed her arm and began dragging her out of the water. She pushed, trying to turn back

34

towards the lake, and was shoved onto the sand. A heavy weight descended onto her and she fought until the white light had bled from her brain, leaving her crumpled and soaked, covered with sand. When she opened her eyes, there was only grey sky and Paul's disbelieving face staring down at her. Mayflies crawled over them both.

'Get off me,' she said.

'D'you know what happens if lightning strikes water while you're in it?' he demanded.

'I said get off me.'

'What were you doing?'

'Get the fuck off!' she yelled.

They stood slowly, fallen trees righting themselves, trunks split open and rotting. She was *so* tired. How was she supposed to explain this?

'Nice scenery,' she said lamely.

Lightning flickered again, illuminating Paul's incredulous face. Without another word, she turned and climbed the path to the ridge, then headed through the endless flutter of wings towards her cabin for a change of clothes.

A bottom corner was wet, but otherwise the photograph was undamaged. Fortunately, Adrien thought, she had tucked her wallet into the pocket of her dad's lumber jacket instead of her jeans. Shivering, she stood in her underwear, observing the smiling faces of her aunt and the eight girls grouped around her. Judging by her aunt's age, the picture was at least two decades old. Were people happier then? she wondered wistfully. The girls' grins seemed impossibly authentic, and each face held its happiness differently. She was sure she had never smiled like that, even before her aneurysm. These days, most teenagers seemed to need group permission to laugh, and then it was a sharp, loud sound that had a manufactured quality, but once she had heard a girl let loose a free sound so startling that Adrien had turned to stare. The girl had looked disappointingly ordinary – brown hair, glasses, pimply skin.

Rain poured steadily, turning the cabin roof and walls into a shell of sound. In the wetness the scent of spruce had sharpened and the air felt deeper, heavier. Hunger hit her in slow waves. How was she going to face Paul? she thought miserably. Would he tell anyone? If only she had thought to sneak some Smarties, she wouldn't have to eat lunch with Aunt Erin and her fan club. Grimly she pulled on a sweater, dry jeans and a raincoat, and headed through the dripping trees to the dining hall.

Predictably, Paul and the two core staff were grouped around Aunt Erin at one of the tables reserved for skills and maintenance staff, while the rest of the dining hall sat empty. Suddenly Adrien was hit with memories of the childhood summers she had spent here, when she had stared at staff tables with a camper's awe, imagining every aspect of the archery instructor's romance with the lifeguard. Back then, staff had seemed like fallen angels – prone to sin and presiding over Camp Lakeshore with heavy wings. She had never before realized they were just older versions of herself. Now *she* would be sitting at one of those tables and some fifth-grade weenie would fall in love with her. The whole thing was an enormous scam. Gloomily Adrien dragged a tray along the serving counter, receiving scoopfuls of macaroni, lime jelly, cucumber salad, and a glass of milk.

'You're lucky,' remonstrated a hairnet, waving her serving ladle. 'We almost went back to where we came from, waiting for you to arrive.'

A hot flush oozed across Adrien's face. Silently she reached for a slice of bread.

'You're missing your smile,' teased another hairnet. 'But Paul here – he's always got a smile for those who feed him, doesn't he?'

Glancing to her right, Adrien saw Paul handing his plate over the counter for seconds. Abruptly she was brushed with the memory of his weight pressing her down on the beach while lightning tore at the sky, but in this vision electricity was also shooting into their mouths – they were breathing white fire. Then the image faded, leaving her open-mouthed, unsure if she had gasped or cried out. Oblivious, the hairnets babbled on about Paul's smile, but Adrien had a feeling he had picked up on something. Maybe the electric current. Well, she thought grumpily, he had better not misinterpret it – she wasn't a weenie camper any more. Picking up her tray, she scuffed towards the only occupied staff table. There, next to Aunt Erin, was an empty space where Paul obviously belonged, so she sat at the opposite end where things would be quieter, less subject to electric visions and unreasonable heart-beats.

Rain pounded the roof. Through the dining hall windows, lightning could be seen lacing the sky, followed almost immediately by thunder so loud it seemed to rise out of the ground. No one reacted. In the quiet aftermath, Aunt Erin made a comment and the core staff laughed. They looked married, as in recently. Adrien glanced at the woman's hands and noticed an engagement ring. No wonder they liked Aunt Erin, she thought. They were in a state of premarital bliss.

Returning from the serving counter, Paul slid his plate onto the table across from her. 'Pass my milk and cutlery,' he called to Aunt Erin through yet another volley of laughter.

Faces turned in his direction, eyes flicked between him and Adrien, an eyebrow lifted. 'Getting a head start, Paul?' asked the groom-to-be, a tall, skinny guy with a black cowboy hat.

Careful as a curler, Aunt Erin slid Paul's knife, fork and glass of milk down the middle of the table, then returned to her macaroni without giving her niece a glance. Startled, Adrien felt as if her face had been erased, as if she didn't exist, as if she had died. Suddenly she hated her aunt. The feeling was like two hands grabbing her stomach and twisting it.

'Are you Adrien?' asked a voice. It was the young woman with the engagement ring. She was plump, friendly-looking, with dark shoulder-length hair. 'I'm Gwen and this is my fiancé Guy. I remember when you were seven years old, building your first fire with tiny little twigs for your Camp-fire badge.'

'Oh yeah,' mumbled Adrien. She didn't like the idea of strangers remembering things about her that she couldn't remember. And she could feel Paul watching her again, his sixth sense scanning the air for trouble. At the other end of the table, Aunt Erin got to her feet.

'I'll be up at the corrals if anyone needs me,' she said. 'You all know what you're doing this afternoon.'

It was an order, not a question. 'Aye-aye, boss,' grinned Guy.

'Adrien, you keep on with inventory. I'll be back to check on things around three.' As Aunt Erin picked up her tray and headed across the dining hall, her thin, lanky body was cast into sharp relief by a bolt of lightning that engulfed the windows. Abruptly everything was reduced to black and white, the hairnets giving a soundless cry as thunder crashed down around the buildings, then faded into a long stretched-out silence.

'Tree on fire!' shouted Aunt Erin, running for the door.

Paul and Guy erupted from their chairs.

'Which tree?' cried Gwen, going after them. 'Please, please don't let it be the Wishing Tree.'

Grabbing her raincoat, Adrien jammed her arms into the sleeves as she passed through the open doorway into midday darkness. Rain was coming down hard – whichever tree had caught fire wouldn't burn long. Head down, she followed Gwen into the woods, and

39

sure enough, when they reached the others, the struck tree was smouldering but there were no flames.

'It is the Wishing Tree,' Gwen wailed.

In the clearing ahead of them stood a huge silver birch. The lightning strike had split it down the middle, leaving one half upright while the other lay on the ground, exposing its blackened gut. Slight whiffs of smoke rose delicately from the charred wood. Placing a hand on the split trunk, Aunt Erin stood silently in the pouring rain, not bothering to pull up her hood. Guy put his arm around Gwen and she leaned against him.

In the wet and dark, nothing moved except the memories in Adrien's head. Every summer she had spent here, her counsellor had woken the cabin of girls in the middle of the night and taken them to see the Wishing Tree. It had always been a night full of moonlight, the Wishing Tree's silvery trunk rising before them like a glowing earth spirit, summoning them into the whispering promise of its leaves. Every counsellor held the ceremony differently: sometimes the girls stood in a circle, sometimes they found private places to sit and watch the tree, but at some point each one touched the tree's shimmering bark and made a wish. That was the magic of it – a girl gave the tree a touch of herself, and it touched her too. Adrien remembered sending something into the silver bark, and the cool green wish the tree had slipped back to her. Now, in the rain, she stepped forward to touch the tree again, send one last wish into its dying life, but as she reached towards the warm trunk Aunt Erin grabbed her hand and pulled it away.

'You've brought something with you, girl,' she said fiercely, the lines of her face made harsher by the rain. 'I don't know the meaning of it, but you be careful what you do here. You just be careful with what's mine.'

Turning, she headed into the trees, her yellow jacket floating in the dark. Lightning flashed and distant thunder rolled. Guy cleared his throat uncomfortably, Gwen patted the tree and made soothing noises, but Adrien stood staring after the disappearing jacket. As the first shock of her aunt's words dissipated, something new began to grow inside her. It was true, she realized. She had brought something to Camp Lakeshore. The spirits on the lake, the storm, the split tree – in some way it all belonged to her. Far across the horizon, the last flicker of lightning danced through her brain, a promise of what was to come.

'Erin's upset. I'm sure she didn't mean that,' Gwen said comfortingly, and Adrien turned back to the others, meeting their eyes one by one. It was easy; at this moment she felt powerful, made of deep, dark earth, wet, whispering trees, huge sky. In response, Gwen blinked, Guy cleared his throat. Only Paul met her eyes, steady and silent.

'Of course she did,' said Adrien, then turned and headed into the trees. She had lunch to eat and a lot of ugly T-shirts to count. After that, an entire summer stretched ahead of her, a summer in which the earth would contain her, the sky hold her close, and her sisters would kick ass on the lake. She might live longer than the end of August, she might not, but if the Big

One got her here, she would die in a place that knew and claimed her as its own.

The evening air held the coolness that followed rain. Bird song ricocheted through the trees. In the middle of unpacking her suitcase, Adrien stopped and listened as cowboy boots stepped onto the cabin's small porch and the outer door opened.

'Adrien?' called a voice. 'It's me.'

Me about summed it up for Aunt Erin, thought Adrien. She stood silently and waited as the boots came down the hall. Her light was on and the door stood open. Anyone with a forty-watt brain could tell she was here. Within seconds her aunt stopped in the doorway, yellow jacket dripping onto the floor. Bug wings clung to the wet material, opening and closing. Without speaking, Adrien folded a sweatshirt and put it in a dresser drawer. It wasn't a Camp Lakeshore sweatshirt.

'Leave the mayflies outside,' she said carefully.

'They'll leave with me when I go.'

'They give me the creeps. You should spray pesticide to get rid of them.'

'Part of the beauty of life,' said her aunt. Raising an arm, she observed the scattering of pale bugs. 'Laid as an egg in the water, live for two years in the lake, then get their full wings and fly for one or two days. Harmless, don't bite, don't even eat once they're flying. Just mate, spawn and die.'

'Two years as an egg so they can fly for two days?' said Adrien. 'What a waste.'

'Spend two years dreaming in the water so they can make their two days in the air worth it. Each second is full of mystery, things you know nothing about. If we spent more time dreaming, maybe we'd have wings too.' Aunt Erin studied the bugs on her arm as if they were her dearest friends. 'Correct term for them is *Ephemeroptera*. Comes from the Greek word *ephemeros*. Greeks made up that word after seeing the way these creatures live. Admired their ephemeral nature.' Her voice held an odd note, as if straining against something. She looked towards Adrien, who glanced away.

'Sorry about what I said this afternoon,' said Aunt Erin, her voice abrupt as ever. 'Shouldn't have said it. Upset about the tree.'

'The Wishing Tree,' Adrien said softly, folding a T-shirt. It wasn't a Camp Lakeshore T-shirt.

'Tree's older than me,' said Aunt Erin. 'Older than the camp. Thousands of kids have wished upon it.'

'Maybe it'll live.'

'Lightning struck its heart. Won't last long.' Her aunt shuffled her feet. It had been almost eight hours since Adrien had seen her. She hadn't come into the office that afternoon, nor had she joined staff members for supper. 'Everything all right?' she asked vaguely.

'Yes,' said Adrien. She started pulling underwear out of her suitcase, all of it labelled with her name so that laundry staff could identify it and return it to her. There was a pause as Aunt Erin hesitated, then sat on the other bed.

'You know summer staff will arrive tomorrow for Training Session?'

'Yes.'

'Your roommate was on staff last summer,' said Aunt Erin. 'She'll teach you the ropes. I expect you to participate in all staff training exercises. Good for you to know what goes on all over the camp. During Training Session, Tuck-'n'-Tack is open from four to five daily for staff purchases. When the kids arrive, you start working full time.'

'Sure.'

'You're here for a reason.' Her aunt still hadn't looked directly at her. 'Don't know why, just felt you needed to be here now. Something to do with you, something to do with the camp.' She paused and rubbed her forehead. 'Won't have much time for you. Camp gets real busy.'

'I know,' said Adrien.

'Just wanted you to know you're welcome. I invited you because I wanted you here.'

'Sure,' said Adrien carefully. If her aunt was going to try for tears and a hugging scene, Adrien was ready to shove her into eternity. Slowly Aunt Erin stood and turned to go, then turned back. In the over-lit room, the bones of her face seemed too large, like an Inuit sculpture.

'Need to ask you this,' she said briskly. Her pale blue eyes fixed on a spot to the right of Adrien's head. 'I'm missing something. A photograph.'

Adrien swallowed, the movement hooking her throat.

'An old picture,' Aunt Erin explained. 'Me and some

kids when I worked here as a counsellor.'

Adrien's hands were shaking. She hid them in her suitcase.

'It's important,' said her aunt. 'Let me know if you find it.'

'Sure,' said Adrien, then listened to her aunt's boots walk slowly down the hall. During the conversation, neither had once looked directly at the other. Now, in the empty air, Adrien could hear every drip of water that fell from the restless trees.

Four

Her new roommate arrived early the next morning. Adrien was still somewhere in sleep, floating in an emerald-green ocean, ascending through light that streamed down from the surface. Weightless, suspended in light, she floated without body, history or parents that clung to her with a suffocating hope. There was just the light and the deep echoing sounds the green water made in her ears. Just the light . . .

The cabin's outer door slammed. Adrien's eyes flew open as someone, muttering loudly, began dragging a heavy object down the hall. Then a kick sent the bedroom door hard into the wall and a girl entered butt-first, pulling a duffel bag. A few steps into the room, she stumbled over a pair of loosely tossed jeans and looked up to find Adrien staring at her.

'Oh my God!' she cried, one hand going to her heart. 'Don't scare me like that!'

'I'm not scaring you,' said Adrien.

'Yes, you are,' said the girl. 'Lying in bed all quiet and sneaky.'

'I was sleeping,' said Adrien. 'I'm a sneaky sleeper.'

The girl gave her a suspicious look, then glanced around the room. 'This place is a mess.'

'Yes, it is,' said Adrien. Locking her hands behind her head, she watched leaf shadows dance across the ceiling. She had to use the bathroom like crazy, but she wasn't giving this girl the satisfaction of knowing it.

'Couldn't you at least have cleaned up before I got here?' the girl asked plaintively. Several years older than Adrien, she was chubby, with carefully curled blonde hair and delicate pink and blue makeup. She looked as if she should be working at some downmarket discount store.

'I was going to clean up when I *got* up,' stressed Adrien.

'Well, *get* up,' said the girl, grunting as she lugged the duffel bag, inch by inch, onto the other bed.

Laundry staff, Adrien guessed, studying her. *On a brave day, arts and crafts.* She could just see this girl gluing coloured macaroni onto glitter-painted cardboard.

'My name's Darcie,' said the girl. She began tugging savagely at the duffel bag's zipper. 'This damn thing's stuck. It's my brother's, he uses it for hockey. It stank so bad, I sprayed it with deodorant.'

'That won't help,' said Adrien. 'It's not an armpit.'

'*Anyway*,' stressed Darcie, ignoring Adrien's biological data, 'it's too small, but Mom said I had to learn to live Spartan. She teaches ancient history. I don't think she ever went to camp as a kid – probably read the *Iliad* instead. How's one duffel bag supposed to last me the

47

whole summer? What did you pack your stuff in?'

'A suitcase,' Adrien admitted.

'A suitcase,' Darcie sighed. 'I had to squish things very tiny, then get my brother and his friend to sit on it while I zipped it closed. Ta-da!' She pulled out a curling iron, waved it around, and set it carefully on the dresser.

'What're you doing here this summer?' Adrien couldn't help the note of incredulity in her voice. Her roommate was a cross between Barbie Doll and the Pillsbury Doughboy. *Thank you, Aunt Erin*, she thought.

'I'm the archery instructor.' Darcie said it with pride.

'You shoot arrows?' Adrien sat up.

'Good,' said Darcie complacently. 'You know the difference between arrows and bullets.' She pulled out a Camp Lakeshore T-shirt, gave it a sniff and wailed, 'It smells like hockey! I'm going to spend all summer smelling like my brother's jockstrap.'

'Maybe if you spray it with deodorant, Spart,' said Adrien.

Darcie set down the T-shirt and gave her another suspicious look. 'Okay,' she said, 'I can already tell we're like night and day. Your aunt obviously put us together to teach us a lesson.'

'What kind of lesson?'

Darcie waved a vague hand. 'Oh, about each other probably. Humanity. The love of life. She likes to improve people.'

'She probably thought you'd improve me,' said Adrien grudgingly. 'She thinks I'm a bump on a log. A grouch from the swamp. Something that lives in your subconscious and never comes up.'

Darcie grinned, then pulled out a makeup kit and started arranging bottles of nail polish and perfume on the dresser. 'I always had the feeling she thought I was kind of flighty,' she said. 'Like she could never figure out how I learned to shoot. It doesn't go with my hairstyle.'

'You really can shoot, eh?' asked Adrien.

'Win every contest I enter,' said Darcie smugly.

'Way to go, Spart,' said Adrien.

'Up and at 'em, Grouch,' replied Darcie.

All morning long, the parking lot was a bustle of cars as summer staff arrived. Adrien was kept busy working her first shift in Tuck-'n'-Tack, selling Mars Bars and sweatshirts to harassed-looking parents, younger brothers and sisters, and new staff members anxious to become Camp Lakeshore lookalikes. Darcie didn't need to purchase anything – she already had a T-shirt in every available colour.

'Dinky sailing boats, Spart,' Adrien had commented as her roommate donned the blue version.

'Evolve out of the swamp, Grouch,' Darcie had replied. 'Learn social skills.'

Social skills, thought Adrien, as she handed two red sweatshirts to a father of twins, *do not come in my size. Do the dead use social skills? Do the dying? Should I take lessons on how to die politely?*

'I'll take a medium blue sweatshirt and an Oh Henry!,' said an obvious staff member-to-be. Mustering her dying social skills, Adrien handed the staff socialite her new sweatshirt and candy bar, gave change and got a smile ready for the next person in line. It was Paul.

'We don't sell smokes,' she said. 'Not even under the counter.'

He tapped the pocket in his lumber jacket. 'When's your break?'

'The boss hasn't told me.'

'Probably won't get one. Busy day.'

'I'm experiencing a major nicotine withdrawal.'

'Don't worry, I've got them when you need them. Give me a Nibs, will ya?'

'Not one of these wonderful T-shirts?' Adrien noticed he wasn't wearing the Camp Lakeshore logo.

'Got one at home,' said Paul. 'If I wear it here, I get mixed up. Too many people wearing the same thing and I can't remember who's me.' He slid some change onto the counter. 'Don't die before I do, eh?'

She handed him the red liquorice. 'The excitement here is killing me.'

He grinned and was gone. She endured until noon, when Aunt Erin helped her close the awning and lock up Tuck-'n'-Tack. Then they stood on the office porch, watching the last of the parents bid farewell to their off-spring in the parking lot.

'Hey, Grouch!' called a voice. 'Give me a smile.'

Startled, Adrien turned with her aunt to see Darcie holding up a camera. There was a click and she lowered it. 'Well, you made a heroic effort anyway,' she grinned. 'Last picture on my roll. I'll mail it off tomorrow.'

As her roommate left, Adrien took a careful step away from Aunt Erin. She would never have allowed herself to be trapped in a photograph with her aunt if she had seen it coming. Sensing the rejection, Aunt Erin stiffened slightly, then spoke in her usual clipped voice. 'Pizza for lunch,' she said. 'Flo, Di and Jo always make a great pizza for first staff lunch. Camp Lakeshore tradition.'

Adrien shrugged. Pizza was pizza. How could anyone non-Italian claim it as a tradition? She headed to the cabin to wash, then changed her mind and ran towards the lake. It had been a long morning without breaks, and she had been waiting to find out if the spirits would show on a day like today, when the camp was full of people laughing, calling, coming and going.

The spirits were gone. Above Adrien's head the sky was a canvas of fresh blue and a strong wind blew steadily in her face, trying to brush away thoughts of gloom and death. But the sunny view in front of her felt completely wrong, just like the photograph of Aunt Erin and her cabin of girls looked true but was utterly false. The real Aunt Erin wasn't a smiling eighteen-year-old or everyone's favourite camp director, she was a woman who prowled the camp-ground like something out of *Wuthering Heights* – terse, dour, locked into some inner secret. That secret hovered over everyone, tangible but unseen. What was most real about this place was hidden in a second mysterious Camp Lakeshore, one that surrounded Adrien like a fading dream. But whose dream was it?

Abruptly she spotted the five girl-shapes slip-sliding the waves, their glow barely visible in the sunlight.

Relieved, Adrien breathed out long and slow. So they hadn't deserted her. No matter how many people crowded the beach and grounds, no matter how many of them wore Camp Lakeshore T-shirts, the true loneliness of this place would remain, a promise between the spirits and herself.

She turned and headed to the dining hall for pizza.

It didn't take long to figure out she was the youngest staff member. Most of the people crowding the staff tables were in the eighteen to twenty-two range and knew each other from former summers. The jokes being told at her table were all loud and inside. Laughter rolled around like a bowling ball, knocking down everyone except her. Adrien ate in silence until a lull appeared, then lunged for it.

'The Wishing Tree was struck by lightning,' she said, not looking up. 'Last night.'

'The ol' Wishing Tree, eh?' drawled the guy sitting across from her. Dressed in a red Camp Lakeshore T-shirt with cut-off sleeves and an expanded neck hole, he had mastered the art of keeping his biceps perpetually flexed. 'Go up in flames?'

'Split in half,' said Adrien, avoiding his eyes. They were too blue. Briefly she wondered if he wore coloured contact lenses.

'Oooh,' he murmured. 'No more midnight wishes.'

'Now we just have to figure out how to stop the midnight pee trips,' sighed a girl in a University of Saskatchewan Huskies sweatshirt.

'Nothing to drink after high noon,' said the guy. 'On pain of death.' The girls at the table seemed to find this riotously funny and Adrien sat, absorbing this latest truth: the Wishing Tree was another scam, perpetrated on weenies hopeful enough to fall for it.

'But don't you think,' she shot into the beginning of yet another inside joke, 'little kids need that sort of stuff? Half the tree's alive – you can still use it.'

Once again, the very blue eyes across from her settled onto her face. This time, she made herself stare back. The guy looked old enough to be attending university, but he had streaked the top of his hair platinum blond like someone searching for easy popularity. He definitely looked manufactured. 'Who are you?' asked the guy in a careless voice. 'An early camper?'

The Huskies girl tittered and slapped his arm lightly. The guy had a ready-made fan club.

'Where'd you get that cute little T-shirt?' asked Adrien. 'The Jock-for-Brains shop?'

The blue eyes flickered in surprise, then hardened as the guy tilted his chair onto its back legs and focused on her. Suddenly Adrien realized her table was stuck in the middle of a long pause, and no one was going to speak a word until Jock-for-Brains did. Completely by accident, she had stumbled onto some kind of social elite and taken on the guy in charge. Chancing another glance, she found the blue eyes still studying her. Everyone else seemed to have developed a manic fixation on their pizza.

'So I asked you a question,' the guy said finally. 'Who are you?'

'Adrien Wood,' she replied, stretching out the words so she didn't sound too obedient.

'What're you doing here?'

'Tuck-'n'-Tack. I sell T-shirts.' Almost smiling, she tasted the last phrase. For a moment the guy continued to observe her, and then he let his chair drop forward and leaned towards her.

'We'll see how your summer goes for you, Adrien Wood,' he said. Then, standing abruptly, he joined the serving line for more pizza. Gradually the conversation at the table picked up, but no one spoke to Adrien, and when Jock-for-Brains returned, he also ignored her. Well, that was all right with her, she thought. She hadn't been thrilled with the conversation anyway. To quote the hairnets, this was one guy who could go back to where he came from, and further.

The early afternoon was spent on an orienteering exercise that split everyone into small groups and sent them all over the grounds, picking mayflies off their bodies while they explored the camp layout. Gloomily Adrien trailed along behind her group. Trying to give her niece a social edge, Aunt Erin had placed her with several new staff members, but it had backfired miserably. The others were several years older and completely ignored her, so Adrien didn't offer any help solving clues. The group wandered perpetually in the wrong direction, up by the corrals when they should have been east of the Arts and Crafts building, close to the lake. As they straggled past, Adrien caught a glimpse of Paul working on the paddock fence. How come he

54

didn't have to attend Training Session? she wondered. It couldn't be due to his advanced social skills.

'Who's the cute guy?' asked one of the girls.

'The Doomsday Man,' said a guy. 'I heard about him. The guy's hooked on gloom – won't talk, won't smile, won't drink a beer. Lives around here somewhere and works on maintenance – cleans the bathrooms.'

'Too bad,' said the girl. 'I like his butt.'

'Check mine out,' said the guy, offering his, and the giggling girl swatted him. As the group rounded a bend in the trail, Adrien glanced back to see Paul had straightened and was watching her. She stopped, caught in a beam of light descending through the trees, the wings of insects flickering gold-white about her. The distance between them made it too far for words so it was just eyes, the two of them locked into a sudden staring silence that deepened until she could hear the slow pound of her heart. The trees sighed heavily, a horse whickered, the earth let loose a rich, dizzying scent. There was the slight pressure of a mayfly on her wrist, the heat of her sunburnt lips, and then, abruptly, the memory from the beach – the weight of Paul's body, his hands pressing her shoulders, and something else – a scream rising through her so raw it threatened to tear open her face. But she hadn't screamed at the beach, Adrien thought, confused. She was sure she hadn't screamed. Turning, she stumbled after her group, clenching and unclenching her fists until her heart slowed, the scent of the earth receded, and the trees stopped giving their soft, whispering sighs.

Her group came in last, having missed half their clues. Seated behind them, Adrien ignored Aunt Erin's penetrating look. It was late in the afternoon and everyone had gathered in the dining hall for an information session. Gwen and Guy were handing out booklets as Aunt Erin introduced the chain of command: the assistant director Maurice Turcotte and his wife, the nurse, and the hairnets, who smiled and bobbed through a standing ovation. When the applause quietened, Guy was introduced as co-ordinator of skills and maintenance staff, and Gwen as leader of the female counsellors. Adrien stood dutifully to be introduced as Tuck-'n'-Tack staff, and wasn't surprised at the dull looks she received. Then a series of shrill whistles pierced the air and she turned to see Paul, Gwen and Guy leaning forward at the back of the room, their fingers between their lips. Flushing, Adrien sat down quickly, but cheers of 'Adrien, Adrien' began, Guy waving his hat, Paul and Gwen stomping and clapping. Another whistle blasted and Darcie waved at her from across the room.

'As you can see,' said Aunt Erin, 'my niece has developed her own fan club. Be good to her – she controls your daily sugar intake.'

Everyone chuckled agreeably, and then Aunt Erin listed the skills instructors, Darcie beaming like a low-level sun, Jock-for-Brains lifting a casual hand as he was introduced as Connor Evans, waterfront co-ordinator. The rest of the afternoon was spent going over the training manual. No smoking, no alcohol, no drugs, no sex in front of the campers . . . Aunt Erin presented an admirable combo act of wry humour and tough lady, leaving Adrien with the feeling everyone knew it would be better not to break Camp Lakeshore's morality code, or at least not to get caught.

After supper she hung around the evening camp-fire, but once again everyone was older and telling inside jokes. Even eighteen-year-old Darcie had better things to do than talk to a fifteen-year-old weenie. So after a phone call home to let her parents know the Big One hadn't hit yet, Adrien headed to bed early.

At eleven-thirty she half-woke when Darcie stumbled in. Then a few hours later she woke a second time to find a flashlight shining in her face.

'Is this your first year on staff?' asked a voice as the flashlight began repeatedly clicking on and off.

'Huh?' mumbled Adrien, deep in a sleep stupor, the harsh light pulling her in and out of consciousness.

'Is this your first year on staff?' the voice demanded again.

'What is this?' asked Adrien. She pushed herself up onto her elbows, then realized the idiot with the flashlight was a guy and ducked back under the covers, but they were pulled off. Shrinking into herself, she wrapped her arms around her knees.

'Get her a sweatsuit and take her outside,' said the guy, flashing the light at Darcie, who was sitting up in bed. Then the light returned to Adrien, resting full in her face. 'Initiation night for new recruits,' said the voice. 'Be outside in five.' The flashlight clicked off and several figures left the room. In the now-dense darkness, Adrien could hear Darcie moving around.

'C'mon,' said her roommate. 'I set these out for you. Put them on.'

'What's going on?' asked Adrien. She didn't move. She had recognized that voice – it belonged to Jock-for-Brains, officially Connor Evans.

'It's just initiation,' said Darcie. 'I went through it last year. No big deal.'

'Maybe I don't want to be initiated.' Adrien waited but Darcie didn't respond, so she asked hesitantly, 'What do they do?'

'You'll see,' said Darcie. 'Put these on. No, don't turn on the light.'

'Why not?'

'It's part of the secrecy of the whole thing. The tradition.'

'I don't like traditions.'

'Look, Grouch,' said Darcie. 'Traditions are what make you part of a group. D'you want to be part of the group, or d'you want to be a reject?'

'I want', grumbled Adrien, 'to go back to sleep.'

But, she admitted unwillingly to herself, Darcie seemed to have survived her initiation. In fact she had become quite a social success, so Adrien finally put on the sweatsuit and trainers she was handed, and followed her roommate outside to where the rest of the cabin stood waiting. Without speaking they set off into the woods, travelling away from the dining hall, the office and Aunt Erin's master cabin, on past the boys' cabins and the corrals, and deep into a wooded area Adrien had never seen. The moon was clouded over, but the girl leading them had a small flashlight and was checking for strips of white cloth that had been tied to trees. Gradually Adrien realized they were moving in concentric circles, but when she pointed this out, she was immediately shushed.

After about twenty minutes, a light could be seen flickering through the trees. There were voices, the odd burst of laughter. Adrien smelled smoke. As they emerged into a clearing, she saw a small fire in a ring of stones, a spot that had obviously been used many times. Why had she never seen this place? she wondered in amazement. Off to one side was a stack of beer, and the clearing was crowded with summer staff, milling around and drinking, laughing and talking in low voices. No one from the upper chain of command was present – not Gwen or Guy, the assistant director or the nurse. When the new arrivals were noticed, cans of beer were opened and handed to them. Remembering her experience at school, Adrien tried to hand hers back, but was refused.

'Free beer,' a guy told her enthusiastically. 'Part of initiation. Chug-a-lug.'

Pulling back into the crowd, Adrien set down her can. She felt safe enough – for once it was an advantage to be an unnoticed weenie – and the party's purpose seemed to be nothing more than breaking the no-drinking and no-smoking rules. But then Connor Evans stepped onto a tree stump and gave a short whistle, his voice cutting into a sudden silence. 'All new recruits step forward,' he said.

His platinum hair glowed eerily in the firelight. Right away Adrien resented his tone of command, but joined the new staff members standing close to the fire. There were sixteen of them, mostly guys, and they made up approximately one-third of the number present. *Why don't we just say no?* Adrien wondered. *There are too many of us to force into anything.* But then she noticed that the guy next to her was unsteady on his feet, and the smell of alcohol hung like a thick fog over everything. She was probably the only one who hadn't drunk at least one beer. This, she thought grimly, might have been a mistake.

'Welcome to your first summer at Camp Lakeshore,' proclaimed Connor.

A burst of guffaws greeted this announcement, followed by a wave of over-emphatic shushing. Connor held up both hands and everyone fell silent.

'A long time ago,' he began, 'when you were all eensy-weensy little buggers in your beds, a tradition was started at Camp Lakeshore. This tradition has been honoured by every staff member who's worked here, and it's been passed down through the years without ever being broken. Even camp administration doesn't interfere.' He cracked a grin. 'Though they know they couldn't if they wanted to, eh? They'd have a revolt on their hands!'

A few members of staff did a quick jig, but grew quiet as Connor again raised his hands.

'These are the rules,' he said grandly. 'There are very few, so even your basic minds should get it. Rule number one: during the day, obey the training manual at all times. Follow the orders of Erin Wood, our great and fearless leader.'

His tone of contempt was obvious, and it was enhanced by further guffaws.

'Rule number two,' he continued. 'After beddy-bye, when all the little kiddies are asleep in their beds, slip quietly into the woods to this midnight fire where the wild ones party.' Cheers erupted. Connor waited for silence, then added, 'If you're on skills or maintenance, we'll expect you here every night. If you're a counsellor, wait for the week you rotate onto maintenance or skills. If you've got campers who are reeeeeally sound sleepers, chance it. Rule number three: what goes on here is kept absolutely secret. There's nothing to be afraid of – just good times – but you will never speak of this place, not even among yourselves. Decade after decade, Camp Lakeshore staff have kept this pact. During the day, we are *so* pure. During the day, we act as if nothing is going on. But after beddy-bye, when the stars come out, the training manual is trash.' Connor spat. 'Here, Erin Wood has nothing to say and she knows it.' Throwing back his head, he said, 'Erin Wood,' stamped his foot once, and grunted.

There were a few soft cheers, and then Connor raised a flashlight and played it over the faces of the new members of staff. 'We have someone special with us tonight,' he said. 'A new recruit who happens to be the niece of our beloved leader, Erin Wood.' Again, he did the stomp-grunt combo, then added, 'A sweet young thing by the name of Adrien.' The flashlight beam passed over Adrien's face and came back to it. 'The Tuck-'n'-Tack girl,' said Connor in a singsong voice. 'Answer me, honey – are you the niece of Erin Wood?'

Adrien hesitated as several staff stamped and grunted. She wasn't her aunt's biggest fan – she knew that – but still, Aunt Erin didn't deserve to have her head repeatedly stamped on by assholes, even as a metaphor. But what to do about it? And how was she supposed to think straight with a flashlight square in her face and everyone watching, all of them older and well on their way to being drunk?

Don't get smart, she thought to herself. *No one here will protect you from your mouth.*

What for? came the answering thought. *I could be dead tomorrow. I'm supposed to spend my last few hours kissing this guy's ass?*

'Yeah, Aunt Erin's in my family tree,' she said finally, her voice wobbling. 'So what?'

Connor's eyebrows lifted. 'So you're going to be our special envoy, kiddo,' he said. 'You've got an in with the boss, and you're working in the office. When we need something, you'll get it for us. *Gopher.*'

There were guffaws and cheers. Connor raised a pinkie and the noise subsided.

'No,' Adrien burst out into the silence, her heart pounding so hard, she thought the Big One was starting its final bright explosion. Then, suddenly, she was calm. The difficult part was over, the enormous choice had been made, and she knew who she was again:

Grouch from the swamp. Social reject. The One Preparing For Death.

'This is shit,' she said. Turning from the line of new recruits, she pushed through the others, who shifted to make room as she passed. At the edge of the group, she realized she wouldn't be able to find her way back in the dark. 'I need a flashlight,' she said, and to her surprise she was handed one. After several frantic heartbeats she found the first white ribbon, then the next. Behind her the revelry picked up as initiation rites continued. From a distance it sounded like fun, and here she was, alone with her choice, stumbling through dark trees and cursing herself for shutting herself out. Why had she decided to work at Camp Lakeshore if she wasn't going to get along with anyone? she thought angrily. Would it have been such a big deal to drink a beer and kiss someone's cowboy boot, or whatever stupid ritual they wanted her to perform?

But the stomp-grunt gesture still riled her. Why did they have to attack Aunt Erin behind her back? she wondered. They acted like her biggest fans to her face. As she reached the cabin, Adrien shut off the flashlight, then turned and headed further through the woods to the clearing where the Wishing Tree stood. The moon had come out and the trunk was two beams of silvery light, one rising, one fallen. The leaves on both halves were still green. Surely it would live, she thought, staring at it. More children than ever would leave their wishes here now – every child knew what it meant to have a heart broken. Placing both hands on the standing trunk, Adrien made a wish. Then she knelt and placed her hands on the fallen part and wished again – the same wish.

Something came back to her. Each time she wished, she felt herself washed by a cool, green gentleness – both halves of the tree sending it into her, the standing and the fallen. So this part of Camp Lakeshore wasn't a scam, she thought shakily. Suddenly she wanted to weep, hug the tree, and beg it to live for all the children who would come to it with open hands and broken hearts, looking for someone to bless and understand them.

'Geezzzus, Adrien,' she muttered. 'It's just a tree.' Seated on the fallen half, she leaned her head against the standing trunk, feeling its strength. Before and after, she thought. They were still connected, weren't they? Still one and the same hope?

On her way to the cabin, she could see the spirits' dim glow hovering on the lake. Even from a distance, she felt their slow writhing as if they were part of her – part of the way she breathed and knew things. It was the stamp of finality pulling her away from everyone normal, their good times. She just didn't belong in the land of the living.

Adrien turned and went alone into the empty cabin. When the other girls returned, she pretended to be dead. Darcie pretended right along with her.

Five

The next morning, everyone acted as if nothing had happened.

'Morning, Grouch,' Darcie said as Adrien opened her eyes.

'Morning, Spart,' muttered Adrien, watching her roommate blow-dry her hair. Darcie had, of course, already showered. It looked like she would have her hair curled before Adrien managed to drag herself out of bed.

'So what did you guys do after I left?' Adrien asked casually. Instead of responding, her roommate continued to dry her hair as if she hadn't spoken. Unsure if Darcie had heard the question, Adrien waited until the dryer went off, then said, 'You guys talk about me after I left?'

Angling the curling iron carefully over her left eye, Darcie rolled up a strand of hair. 'What d'you figure we'll be doing today, Grouch?' she asked carelessly. 'More of the training manual, I bet. God, it's boring. I memorized the whole thing last year.'

Adrien jerked herself angrily into a sitting position. 'I asked you about last night,' she spluttered. 'What happened after I left?'

'Left where?' asked Darcie. Well-defined curls were springing up all over her head.

Fear beat a soft drum in Adrien's mouth. 'Why're you doing this?' she whispered. 'What did I ever do to you?'

For a second, Darcie froze. Then a bright, chipper look appeared on her face. 'It's going to be a nice *day*,' she said, stressing the last word. 'I hope you have a great *day* today, Grouch.' Brushing out her curls, she gave herself a satisfied glance in the mirror and pulled on a sweater. 'Breakfast in five. Gotta go.'

'Sure thing, Spart,' Adrien muttered as her roommate went out of the door. 'Don't shoot any broken arrows.'

'Hey, Mira!' Darcie called down the hall. 'Coming for breakfast?'

A sudden bout of whispering could be heard, followed by Darcie's cheerful, reproving voice. 'It's going to be a nice *day*, don't you think, Mira? I hope I can get some practice in at the archery range.'

'Oh yeah,' said Mira loudly, catching on. 'Oh yeah, it's a real nice *day*. I can see it's very sunny and bright out there.'

As the outer door slammed, Adrien sat up grouchily. So, she thought, it looked as if rule number three was going to be strictly obeyed . . . by the obedient. If what Connor had said was true, she was the only disobedient staff member in decades, which left no one else to disobey rule number three with, not even administration

– not that she wanted to run to her aunt and tattle. Well, she could live with ignoring the whole thing as long as they left her alone. All they really wanted was her mouth shut so they could party. They sure weren't interested in her witty companionship or sparkling personality – probably the entire group was vastly relieved that the Doomsday Girl had rejected them.

The morning went by absolutely normally. Everyone was friendly. Connor made a point of saying 'good morning' without evil undertones. In charge of the morning session by the beach, he began with a careful explanation of the waterfront safety regulations. As he spoke, the sunlight enhanced his hair dye, the wind ruffled his golden locks, and his biceps rippled. He was wearing his designer Camp Lakeshore T-shirt, and he was gorgeous.

Adrien didn't see why she had to stand around listening to a hypocrite discuss the *rules* for sailing, so early into Connor's spiel she began edging into the trees, then turned and walked past the girls' cabins and the fenced-off septic tank. Veering left, she steered clear of the archery range, which was never to be approached from the south, and came out of the woods onto the road that led to the corrals. She had and hadn't been thinking about Paul, so when she caught sight of him working on another section of fencing, she was caught in a rush of confusion, wanting and not wanting the feelings that flew through her on raw wings. She was used to the guys at school, but not like this. Not with a slow wind riding the trees, and with the rich, deep smell of earth so strong she could feel it in her skin. He wasn't even close and she felt like they were touching.

'Hey, Angel,' he called.

'I'm not Angel.' Overdoing her anger made it easier to face him. As she approached, he was smiling. So much happened in his face when he smiled. Whole stories told themselves.

'All right, *Adrien*,' he said. 'What're you doing up here?'

'Nothing. Much. Really.' Words weren't doing the sentence thing for her today. Adrien stared intensely at the toe of Paul's boot.

'So help me with this fence. Here, grab this.' He handed her a rail and she held it as he hammered it into place.

'I'm supposed to be at Connor's sailing session,' she said, as if she owed Paul an explanation. 'But –'

'But what?' Paul straightened and looked at her. He was about an inch taller, his eyes brownish-green, his lips a soft flush of red.

'Uh.' She couldn't seem to speak. 'Last night –'

'Initiation?' He turned back to the fence. 'So how'd it go?'

Adrien stared at Paul in astonishment. He was actually breaking rule number three! Finally, a partner in sanity. Her shyness vanished. 'Did you have to do it?' she asked eagerly.

'They tried to make me last summer, but I'm never here at night. Wild man capers with city-slicker tough guys,' he said softly. 'What a blast.'

Adrien hesitated, unsure if he was including her. 'They said Aunt Erin knows about it. I doubt it. She'd never let them get away with breaking all those rules.'

'She knows,' Paul said quietly. 'She used to be summer staff. She went to deep-woods parties twenty years ago.'

Adrien gaped. She could not imagine her aunt doing anything that . . . social. Catching sight of her expression, Paul grinned.

'Who cares what they do?' he asked, 'As long as they don't tear down any buildings or raise the dead.'

'But the training manual says —' started Adrien.

'They show up for their jobs in the morning and treat the kids okay,' Paul broke in. 'It's their business what they do in the middle of the night.'

'Then why don't you go?' demanded Adrien.

'I don't like the company,' he shrugged, then paused. 'What exactly do they do out there, frolicking in the woods?'

'It's not *Lord of the Flies*,' she said. 'There aren't any sticks sharpened at both ends. It's mostly drinking. They make the new members of staff do something stupid, so I left.'

'You don't like parties?' asked Paul.

'I didn't like the way they were talking about Aunt Erin,' she burst out. 'They suck up to her all day, then talk her down when they get out there at night. If they don't like her, they should act like it to her face.'

'Like you do?'

'Yeah.' Adrien looked at him breathlessly, challenging

him to tell her she was wrong. Slowly his eyes moved over her face.

'You want a cigarette?' he asked. 'I get a mid-morning break. C'mon, we'll go into the trees so no one sees us.' Gently he touched her bare arm and she almost cried out at the sudden heat.

'Um, here's fine,' she said. 'I, uh, like the horses.'

His smile faded. 'Sure. We'll watch the horses.' Fishing the pack out of his lumber jacket, he handed her a cigarette. 'Careful,' he said, raising an eyebrow. 'Smoking kills ten out of ten, y'know.'

'D'you really believe', she asked carefully, 'that you know exactly when and where you're going to die?'

He gave a short laugh and leaned on the fence, watching the horses at the other end of the paddock. After a pause, she realized that had been his response.

'Well, aren't you going to do something about it?' she demanded. 'Make sure it doesn't happen?'

'What're you doing about yours?' he asked, not looking at her.

'I can't do anything,' she snapped. 'It's my brain. My blood vessels are warped. Yours aren't.'

He stared moodily into the trees. 'It's going to happen, one way or another.'

'That's an attitude,' she said flatly.

'Oh yeah?' He turned to look at her, his face derisive. 'You're telling me I've been dreaming an *attitude* for two years? It's my *attitude* that keeps killing me a hundred different ways? You're telling me my *attitude* put you in my dreams before I ever saw or heard about you?'

He was so intense, the air about him throbbed. 'No,' she stammered, almost frightened, 'that's not what I meant.'

'Good,' he said tersely. 'I've got to get back to work.'

Ducking through the rails, he left her standing alone with her cigarette.

The girls in the photograph could have been from her classes at school, she thought, studying it. Swimsuits hadn't changed that much since the 1970s, and neither had hairstyles. Where had they come from, she wondered, and what had they returned to after their week at camp? Had Camp Lakeshore changed their lives – brought the shy ones out of their shells and taught the arrogant ones a lesson? Had they all made wishes at the Wishing Tree and had their wishes come true? They would be adults now, old enough to be her mother. How many of their children had experienced a brain aneurysm? Had any of them died?

It was Friday morning, the last day of Training Session. Alone in the cabin, Adrien was sitting on her bed, skipping yet another staff activity. The only workshops she had attended all week had been led by Aunt Erin, Guy or Gwen, because they were the only instructors who would have noticed or cared about her absence. The lesson she was currently skipping dealt with wilderness camping, and was full of exciting scenarios such as where to set a tent on the side of a hill in a swarm of soldier ants with a storm brewing. After lunch, Connor would be leading a session on staff morale. Adrien had seen the list of exercises on Aunt Erin's desk. The first one involved standing on a fence post and falling backwards into the arms of fellow staff members. Bonding was supposed to occur *if* they caught and cradled you. Fat chance she was showing up for that one.

Paul hadn't spoken to her since her killer comment about his attitude problem. Every time he saw her, a dark mood swallowed his face and he turned away. The guy could sure hold a grudge – her nicotine withdrawal was driving her up the wall.

Darcie spoke to her only in passing. Several times during the week, Adrien had woken in the middle of the night to see her roommate heading out or coming back in, but she didn't ask questions and Darcie didn't discuss anything. If staff looked suspiciously hung over in the morning, Aunt Erin didn't mention it. *Maybe she's used to it*, Adrien thought. *Maybe she always lets them party-hearty during Training Session.* Tomorrow, staff got the day off, and on Sunday the first wave of campers were to arrive. Aunt Erin probably realized the night frolics would eventually fizzle out from sheer exhaustion.

Adrien was tired of trying to figure it all out. She was tired of everyone walking by with chipper smiles, tossing words at her that were supposed to matter. 'Hey, Grouch! How's it going, Grouch?' No one waited for an answer – they all hurried off to another workshop, the essential training manual tucked under an arm. *Hypocrites*, Adrien thought bitterly. The whole place was a scam. If she reached out and actually touched some-one, the person would probably dissolve into mist and fade away.

The only place she felt solid was standing by the lakeshore, watching the spirits. Over the past few days, their glow had been growing brighter. She had been checking several times daily and they were always there, floating on the water's surface. Watching them she felt at peace, drifting in a dream as vast as the lake and lis-tening to the thousand tiny waves of her heart.

Intently she leaned over the photograph, focusing on the five girls who clustered so close to Aunt Erin they seemed like a single unit. They were the ones with the social telepathy, she thought knowingly – the girls who walked through a cabin door, scanned everyone, and immediately recognized those who would become life-long friends. Until her aneurysm, Adrien had fitted right in with these girls. She had never given a second thought to the stragglers, the outsiders. Now she looked at the three girls standing back from the group. Their smiles were wistful – they weren't so sure they were happy. Each carried a visible strike against her: two were chubby, one had braces, another wore glasses. In contrast, the girls at the centre of the photograph looked as if they rode a constant ongoing laugh – all they had to do was glance at each other and the giggles would burst free, creating a separate universe to which only they belonged.

The girl under Aunt Erin's left arm was probably the leader, Adrien decided. She had black shoulder-length hair and her nose was slightly beaked, but she was still pretty and she knew it. As she gazed into the camera, her mouth was wide open; she looked loud, friendly, and entirely oblivious to the existence of the three wistful girls in the background. She looked like every best friend Adrien had made during her Camp Lakeshore summers.

Without warning, the cabin turned cold. A slight wind picked up, something different coming through the trees. In one corner of the room a faint blur shifted, and a shiver ran down the back of Adrien's neck. Her breath stilled. Slowly she raised her eyes, but the room remained empty of anything but the whispering green light. Whatever had just come from between the worlds to watch her was gone, but she knew it had been there. When she breathed again she breathed deeper, as if the air also came from a place beyond this one and she was breathing it in, pulling other worlds closer, until finally she would be able to see them and understand.

Leaned against the fence at the archery range, Adrien watched her roommate. Darcie's hair was perfectly curled and her neon-blue makeup glowed, but that didn't detract from the whistle she wore around her neck and the way she was speaking with *the voice of authority*.

'*No one,*' Darcie said emphatically, 'absolutely *no one* is to step across this shooting line for any reason until I blow the whistle. If you notch your arrow improperly and it falls to the ground in front of you instead of flying through the air, too bad. Sometimes arrows from other people's bows fly sideways, and you can get hit just leaning over the line. If you're the stupid sucker who wastes a shot, leave it on the ground. If I catch you crossing that line, even *leaning* over it before I blow my whistle, you'll lose shooting privileges, got it?'

It was mid-afternoon. Connor had finished his morale booster, and staff members had gathered for the last workshop of Training Session, the only one Adrien had actually been interested in attending. Hiding a grin, she continued to watch as Darcie glared ferociously at the group, trying to imprint on them the seriousness of the situation. 'Grade five and six girls are the *worst*,' she said with disgust. 'They get the giggles and forget they've got a loaded bow. Someone makes a joke and they turn around to hear it.' Darcie illustrated, whirling suddenly and pointing a loaded bow at the startled crowd. 'If you've got a cabin of gigglers,' she warned, 'you're going to have to give them a serious talk before they get here. I don't tolerate gigglers on my range. Understood?'

When enough staff had nodded, Darcie stopped pointing her loaded bow at them and moved into the proper stance for loading and shooting. Targets had been pinned to four straw bales at the opposite end of the range. They looked a long way off, and Adrien watched in disbelief as her roommate's first arrow sailed through the air, burying itself in a bull's-eye. The group's mild clapping grew louder as Darcie repeated this act with her second and third arrows. 'It's a short range,' she said dismissively. 'It's not hard to hit the target unless it's windy. It's for kids, after all.'

The group split into four lines, and Darcie handed three arrows to the first person in each line. At the back of her line, Adrien watched as arrows began wobbling, wiggling and whizzing through the air. Cheers and whistles accompanied the odd bull's-eye, but no one managed consecutive ones, not even Connor, who went first and hit the target every time. Once all twelve arrows had been released, Darcie blew her whistle, and the archers retrieved their arrows and handed them to the next person in line. Then Darcie wailed on her whistle and another round of shooting began.

Adrien managed to land her first arrow on the target's outer ring. Her next shot arced high and nose-dived, embedding itself in the ground. Her third flew over the back fence into the trees. 'Way to go, Grouch,' called the staff members in her line, and turned back to their private conversations. Surrounded and alone, Adrien waited for Darcie's manic whistle, then headed onto the range with the other archers. Her first two arrows were easy to find, but the third was going to be difficult – the feathers that identified her set of arrows were green. Passing through the gate at the back of the range, Adrien pushed into the mass of green shrubbery ahead of her. Had her dumb green arrow gone high or low when it zoomed over the fence? she wondered. Had it disappeared into this green bunch of leaves or that green bunch? Behind her, she could hear staff pulling their arrows out of the targets and making jokes about being reincarnated as Robin Hood. 'Get this,' proclaimed one guy. 'Robin Hood gets reincarnated as *me*.'

Boos and hisses accompanied this comment. Reluctantly Adrien pushed further into the greenery. Darcie had been adamant about returning with all three arrows. They were expensive to replace, and it taught *responsibility*. Grumpily, Adrien pushed onward through mosquitoes and poison ivy until her responsible foot knocked against the missing arrow. With her incredible skill and accuracy, she had managed to hit the ground twice. As she bent down to retrieve it, she noticed a yellow arrow embedded near by. Feeling doubly responsible, she pulled them both out, then returned to the gate at the south end of the range and pushed it open.

Arrows were coming straight at her. With a scream, Adrien ducked behind the nearest straw bale. There was a thump as an arrow hit the other side, and she jerked back. Her heart thudded, the whole world squeezed in and out of darkness; she could hear whimpering sounds and a far-off whistle. Then the air grew oddly quiet. Footsteps came running towards her, and Darcie stepped behind the bale.

'You all right?' she cried, panting. 'Grouch, did you get hit?'

Adrien crouched wordless, arms tight around herself. She couldn't stop shaking, even when Darcie knelt and hugged her. *Everyone* had been shooting at her. Everyone had been shooting at *her*.

'Some safety procedures,' she hissed.

'It was an accident,' said Darcie. 'You took so long, I forgot you were out there.'

'My group didn't have their arrows,' said Adrien.

'They knew I was out there. Why didn't they say something?'

Darcie's perfume was suffocating. Adrien wanted to pull away but couldn't. Not yet.

'I don't know,' Darcie said uncomfortably, 'but I'm the one in charge. I'm the one who let them shoot. It was an accident. I'm sorry, Grouch. I really am.'

Darcie's apology was absolute and so was her hug. Safe and warm inside that hug, Adrien still couldn't stop thinking about Connor. While she was out looking for her lost arrow, he had been rotating to the front of his line for a second round. And in that split second before Adrien had realized there were three loaded bows pointed in her direction, she had got a clear glimpse of his smirk. It had been obvious to her even then, that he had just caught sight of her coming through the south gate, and was shifting his bow from a target to her face.

It took Aunt Erin all of two seconds to notice the scrape on her niece's upper arm. 'You get that at the range?' she asked immediately.

Picking up the till to carry it out to Tuck-'n'-Tack for staff candy hour, Adrien avoided her aunt's gaze. 'Get what?' she asked vaguely.

She refused to think about the range. Huge hollow caves still echoed in her knees and gut. Aunt Erin came over and ran her finger over the scrape.

'Ow!' Adrien hissed.

'Arrow burn,' said her aunt. 'How'd this happen?'

'It didn't,' said Adrien. 'All right?'

Aunt Erin's voice was loaded. 'You put down that till and talk.'

Suddenly, holding onto the till took on overwhelming significance. Rigid, Adrien stared out of the screen door. Clouds were building over the lake. 'I bumped into a tree branch while I was looking for an arrow,' she said. 'I didn't even notice my arm until you poked it.'

In her mind's eye, she kept seeing Connor's smirk. If she told Aunt Erin what had happened, Darcie was the one who would get into trouble, not him. And it hadn't been Darcie's fault. Darcie had hugged her in front of the rest of the staff. She had hugged and hugged Adrien, helped her to her feet, and walked back to the group with an arm around her, keeping her so close Adrien had felt her roommate's heart beat.

Had Connor's arrow been the one to graze her arm? *Had it?*

'I've got the rest of the afternoon,' said Aunt Erin, folding her arms and parking her butt on the edge of her desk. 'And so do you.'

Holding onto the till, Adrien stared at the bare wood floor. Outside, the wind grew louder, everywhere in the trees. Aunt Erin switched on the PA. 'Darcie Smythe to the office,' she said. 'Darcie Smythe.'

They waited in silence. *I could call Mom and Dad*, Adrien thought. *I could just go home.* But outside she could feel the clouds building on the lake like a promise. The sound of the wind moved through her as if she was part of its message, leaves lifting and falling inside her, whispering their meanings. Gradually the shaky,

79

hollow feeling within her faded and she felt part of this place, older than anything that could happen to her here, just like the trees, the lake, and the sky were older than the camp. People were small stories that the wind blew clean, she thought, and then they were forgotten. One day, her story would be blown across the lake and she would be forgotten too. This didn't frighten her.

A shadow shifted through a patch of light on the floor, a writhing shape that lifted its arms to her, then faded. Quickly Adrien glanced at her aunt, but she was staring grimly at the door and hadn't seen the spirit. She also hadn't noticed that the clock above her desk had stopped at one thirty-seven. Adrien glanced at the clock on the opposite wall. It said three fifty-five.

'Your clock stopped,' said Adrien.

Aunt Erin glanced automatically at the clock. Then, as Adrien watched in astonishment, her aunt lost the tight grip she usually kept on her face and stared in absolute fear. Abruptly her expression closed over again. 'Acting up, is it?' she muttered, moving towards it as the first sound of Darcie's footsteps started up the porch stairs. A slumped figure appeared in the doorway.

'Come in,' said Aunt Erin, her voice even, her pale eyes icy. Darcie took one step through the doorway and waited.

'Explain the arrow burn on my niece's arm,' said Aunt Erin.

'It's not —' began Adrien.

'Yes, it is,' Darcie said miserably.

'Adrien kept her mouth shut. Didn't betray you,' said

Aunt Erin. 'Not her fault I'm firing you.'

'What?' gasped Adrien.

Blinking hard, Darcie stared at the dead clock. Then she nodded and turned to go. 'Don't you even want to hear what happened?' demanded Adrien.

'Want a full explanation,' said Aunt Erin. 'But Darcie's fired just the same.'

Facing the door, Darcie explained. Then she walked out. The screen door slammed behind her.

'Open Tuck-'n'-Tack,' said Aunt Erin. Walking over to the clock, she began to fix it.

'No,' said Adrien. 'I quit. I'm going home.'

'Suit yourself,' said Aunt Erin.

'I'm not suiting myself,' hissed Adrien. 'I *hate* you. You never give anyone a second chance. Darcie would never let it happen again.'

'Could've been killed,' said Aunt Erin, her eyes bright. 'Don't get second chances when someone's dead.'

'I'm not dead!' yelled Adrien. 'No stupid arrow's going to kill me – you know that. I'll die the way I'm going to die, and nothing's going to stop it. You could fire a million staff and nothing would stop it.'

'Got nothing to do with it,' snapped Aunt Erin. 'Her carelessness almost got someone killed.'

'None of them can shoot,' howled Adrien. 'Only Darcie can aim and she wasn't shooting.'

'Got your arm,' said Aunt Erin.

'Lucky chance,' said Adrien, stamping on the floor. 'You make me so mad. Give her a break. That stupid archery range'll be safer than a daycare after this.'

Aunt Erin sat down quietly on the edge of the desk. Abruptly Adrien realized how closely she was being watched.

'You like rooming with Darcie?' Aunt Erin asked.

'She's all right,' Adrien said grudgingly. 'I never knew Robin Hood wore nail polish.'

Aunt Erin cracked a slow smile and rocked once. Head back, she took a deep breath and her face relaxed. 'Maybe I was too hasty,' she said. 'You find Darcie and tell her to come and talk to me.'

'You won't fire her?' squeaked Adrien.

'We'll work things out,' said Aunt Erin. Her eyes had taken on a whole different shade of pale blue. The ice was melting.

'THANKS!' shouted Adrien. Dumping the till, she raced to the door.

'Oh, and Adrien,' called Aunt Erin.

'What?' asked Adrien, turning back.

'You give life a second chance too,' said Aunt Erin.

Six

Later that afternoon, Adrien was wandering through the wooded area surrounding the cabins set aside for the older girls. She wanted to go down by the lake, but a quick glance had shown Connor and a few others ignoring the cloud cover and getting into canoes for a paddle before supper. According to the staff schedule, she was supposed to be working in Tuck-'n'-Tack, but she couldn't get at the key or the till because Darcie was in the office talking to Aunt Erin. A *DO NOT DISTURB* sign had been posted on the door.

The mayflies were definitely dying off. It was the last Friday in June and the ground was littered with their brown, withered bodies. Grimacing slightly, Adrien pulled seven live ones off her shirt and watched them flutter away. At the start of Training Session, it would have been twenty-five. In just over a week, they would all be gone.

Abruptly, to her right, she heard voices and laughter coming from the cabin that was called Prairie Sky. Startled, Adrien came to a halt. These cabins were supposed to be empty until Sunday, when the campers arrived, but as she listened, another peal of laughter floated out of a window. Prairie Sky was the cabin closest to the lake, the only one in this section she had never stayed in. Still, she knew what it would look like. Each cabin held five bunk beds and several dressers. Upon her arrival she had always grabbed a top bunk and spent her week sleeping mid-air, drifting on the ebb and flow of the other girls' breathing.

The cabin's windows were open, airing the place out. Standing on tiptoe, she could just see in. At first there was nothing out of the ordinary, just the quiet green light filtering through the trees. But then she glimpsed something in a corner – someone turning, part of her visible but transparent. With a soft gasp, Adrien recognized the girl from Aunt Erin's photograph, the one with the beaked nose and the wide, laughing mouth. She was laughing now, her voice clear, and then she spoke.

'What would Erin do if she knew we were spying on the guys' cabins?' she asked

'She'd probably want to come along,' replied a second girl as she came into view, also transparent but easily recognizable with her long red ponytail, tube top and shorts – another of the five girls that had been grouped close to Aunt Erin. 'Especially if we picked Spruce Hollow,' the girl added with a grin. 'Sure wish we had Peter Pecker for our counsellor. Think he could wear tighter swim trunks?'

'Not and still get into them.' This voice belonged to

a girl sitting on a top bunk. All Adrien could see of her were vague swinging legs.

'You think Erin will get into them?' asked the first girl.

Another peal of laughter erupted.

'She's sure been watching him,' said a fourth voice, out of Adrien's line of sight. 'I was almost drowning at swim class yesterday, and she didn't even notice.'

'We should set them up,' said the first girl. Arms out-stretched, she spun a thoughtful pirouette. 'Then spy on them. I'd give them twenty minutes to complete the dirty deed.'

'You only need three.' With this comment, another girl walked into view. The last of the photograph's laughing group of five, she had short blonde-brown hair with obvious highlights, and was pulling on a swimsuit, careless of who watched.

'*You* only need three, Nat,' said the first girl, stopping her pirouette. 'Most people do more than grunt and jump on each other, you know. Erin would want time to . . . ease into it.'

More giggles erupted. The girl with the swinging legs fell backwards, kicking her legs in glee.

'How would you know?' asked Nat, now fully dressed and fluffing her hair. 'I'm the only one here who's done it.'

'Yeah, you did it,' said the first girl. 'But did you enjoy it? That's what I'd like to know.'

Nat ignored her.

The legs resumed their swinging. 'D'you think he'd kiss her first, or would she kiss him?'

'He'd kiss her.' Nat's reply was automatic.

'D'you think he'd touch her boobs?' asked the legs.

'If they were going to get anywhere,' said Nat.

Still peering through the window, Adrien could feel herself getting hot and bothered. She hadn't had girlfriends since she was thirteen, when French kissing had been the hot topic. There had been jokes about groping, sure, but no one had been this graphic about what came after.

'D'you think she'd touch his —'

Without warning, the voices and outlines of the girls vanished, and Adrien whimpered in disappointment. Just when it had been getting interesting. And they had been talking about *Aunt Erin*.

'Watching the dead?' asked a voice to her left.

Adrien whirled. There, in the clearing at the front of the cabin stood Paul, holding a dark brown bottle. Heart pounding, she sagged against the cabin wall.

'Don't sneak up on me like that,' she snapped.

'Sorry,' he said. 'That cabin's haunted. See any ghosts?'

'No,' she said immediately. 'I stayed in this cabin once. Nostalgia, you know.'

'Door's open,' said Paul. 'Just walk in and get fully nostalgic.'

'In a haunted cabin? No thanks.' She wasn't sure why she was lying. It was just that for the past three years, everything in her life had been private, separate. She had grown used to holding experiences to herself, the way she had clutched the till in Aunt Erin's office. Who would she be if she let go?

'The nurse is off until Sunday, so Erin sent me to doctor you.' Producing a package of cotton wool, Paul unscrewed the bottle cap.

'It's just a scrape,' Adrien said, stepping back.

Paul shrugged. 'Erin's hyper about this kind of stuff. Lose a hangnail, she'll send you to Emergency. C'mon, I just have to clean it, make sure you aren't about to croak.'

'What makes you an expert?'

He made a few harsh croaking noises. 'On the verge.'

Adrien grinned reluctantly, then extended her arm. In spite of Paul's easy conversation, the situation felt awkward, full of echoes: *It's going to happen, one way or another. That's an attitude. It's my attitude that keeps killing me a hundred different ways?*

'How'd you know where I was?' she asked, wincing as the hydrogen peroxide settled into the broken skin.

'Sniffed you out.' Paul leaned close, wiping away a trickle of dry blood. 'I can do that sometimes.'

'Creepy,' said Adrien. 'Aunt Erin says you have a sixth sense.'

'Maybe.' Carefully he swabbed the sore area, examining every stinging millimetre.

Adrien wanted to pull away from the pain, but his dark hair was tickling her cheek, causing her brain to go soft and fuzzy. Suddenly all she wanted to do was smell his hair, to brush her lips across it. She wanted . . .

Paul looked up, his eyes on her slightly open mouth.

'Whose arrow was it?' he asked.

'I don't know.'

'Take a guess.'

'A lot of people were shooting.'

'Adrien,' he said pointedly, 'you get shot by an arrow and you're seeing ghosts. Something's going on here.'

Instantly Adrien's chin went up and she stepped back. 'You don't talk to me for days,' she said, 'and now you think you can just tell me what's going on in my life? I told you, I didn't see any ghosts. And the arrow was an accident.'

'I doubt it.' Paul stepped forward; she took another step back. 'There's a strange light around you,' he said quietly. 'You glow. Like you're standing in the light from some other place.'

She opened her mouth, then closed it. The silence around them was tremendous.

'That first day,' said Paul, 'down by the lake, I saw past you. You were sitting in the lifeguard's chair and just beyond you, in the sky, was a huge opening. There was another world there, full of others. Others who've passed through. They were watching you.'

Abruptly Adrien's head was full of tiny falling things. Turning from his dark, staring eyes, she ran into the whisper of the knowing trees.

She woke suddenly to someone leaning over her in the dark. From the scent of perfume she knew it was Darcie but still Adrien feigned sleep, listening to the other girl's soft, uneven breathing. It was the middle of the night; Darcie had to be either heading out to the camp-fire or coming back in. What could she possibly want now?

88

Adrien wondered. To drag her along a second time? To deliver a nasty message from Connor? After her conversation in the office with Aunt Erin, Darcie had spent the evening camp-fire watching Adrien, her face twisted in thought that was obviously new territory, but the two girls hadn't spoken since Adrien had run into the cabin that afternoon and pulled Darcie's duffel bag out of her hands, panting so hard she could barely get out the words: 'You're not fired. Aunt Erin says she made a mistake. Go and talk to her. Now.' When Darcie had hesitated, a proud grimace on her face, Adrien had burst out with a raw 'Please!'

Why had it mattered so much? she had wondered later. For that second while Darcie had wavered, Adrien had thought her heart would split wide open with panic, but finally the other girl had turned, tight-lipped, and left the cabin. In the empty room Adrien had sunk down onto the bed, next to the pile of makeup and clothing her roommate had been about to shove into the stinky duffel bag, and the next few minutes had been complete exhaustion. When the air had begun to move again, she had put everything away where it belonged: the perfume and nail polish on the dresser, the duffel bag under the bed, the frilly, lacy underwear in the dresser drawers.

Now, in the dark, Darcie's hand brushed her shoulder. Adrien kept her eyes closed.

'You surprised me, Grouch,' said Darcie, her voice whispering within itself, so quiet it was almost thought. 'Your aunt told me what you said. I never would've thought you'd stick up for me. I thought you hated all of us, maybe me the most, but I guess you don't. I guess you really think the camp-fire's stupid. Well, I'm going to tell you something. I think it's stupid too, but I don't have your guts. Or maybe I like people more, I don't know. But from now on, I'm your friend. I'll stick up for you, I promise.' A quiet pause followed, filled with Darcie's soft breathing. Then she straightened and moved to the door. 'One last thing, Grouch,' she added. 'I know you're awake. I know you heard what I just said. When I promise something, I mean it. We're friends, whatever that takes.'

Without waiting for an answer, Darcie slipped out of the door, and Adrien listened to the sounds of the other girls following her. Then they were gone, fading into the night, heading off to do whatever it was they did around the camp-fire when Aunt Erin wasn't watching. Motionless, Adrien lay a while longer, then sat up. About her the night air felt full of huge places, shifting and rearranging. That afternoon, talking to Paul, she had been afraid, but now she was restless, stirred by dark currents and far from sleep. Slipping on a pair of jeans and her father's lumber jacket, she left the cabin and headed through the woods towards the lake, then cut across the lawn to the older girls' cabins, just inside the trees.

Dark and silent, Prairie Sky loomed, no transparent girls giggling in their beds. Had they actually been ghosts like Paul had said, she wondered, observing the cabin, or had she imagined them because she had stared so long at the photograph? And why had there only been five girls? Where were the other three Aunt Erin had counselled that week?

The answer came to her as she emerged from the trees onto the ridge above the beach, there in the grey, smoky glow floating on the water's surface – the spirits of five girls splayed as if in sleep. She felt the certainty of it then, like cold water swamping her face. The girls she had seen that afternoon in Prairie Sky were the five girls in her aunt's photograph, and they had all died somehow while they were young. For some mysterious reason their spirits had returned to haunt the lake. But why? she wondered. Were their deaths the reason her aunt prowled the camp-ground in the dark, the reason Adrien had caught her on the beach that first night, staring out at the water? Something connected Aunt Erin to those spirits, and it was more than the fact that she had been their counsellor while they were alive. Why else would she keep a photograph of them under the mat on her desk, where she could slip it out and look at it several times a day? *Don't get second chances when someone's dead*, Adrien remembered her saying. Some deep tragedy had hold of Aunt Erin, a mystery that linked her to the five girls' deaths, something no one ever talked about, including Adrien's parents. If any staff at Camp Lakeshore knew, they were keeping quiet out of respect. The secret had been completely buried, just like the girls' bodies must have been.

But the girls weren't keeping themselves buried. Earlier that evening, at suppertime, Adrien had seen them again, lined up in front of the dining hall, their five faces pretending to be quiet and well-behaved so they could get in for food. There had been just a glimpse, and then they had disappeared. Seconds later, staff members had walked through the place where the girls had been standing without a flicker of awareness, and when Adrien had stepped into it there had been nothing, not even the whisper of a girl's voice, her far-off laughter.

Sitting on the ridge, she watched the spirits. They seemed to be sleeping, drifting on invisible currents but always together, as if they were a single unit. That afternoon, she had heard their voices and learned one of their names. *Nat*, she thought wonderingly. *Short for Natalie?* What were the rest of their names? What were their stories? And why were the girls appearing to her both before and after, alive and dead? They seemed trapped between worlds, unsure where they belonged, just like she was.

The lake lapped at the shore, quiet but uneasy. The ground was covered with dead wings. Abruptly Adrien realized she was probably staining the seat of her jeans and was about to get up when someone sat down beside her, bumping her knee. Turning, she saw Connor, his hair phosphorescent in the moonlight. An immediate coldness crept through her, and she went very still. Some way down the beach, a frog called slow and steady. The moon shone lonely and empty, the silent camp-ground stretched behind them. The rest of the staff would be at the camp-fire now, she thought, but Aunt Erin, Guy and Gwen were near by, sleeping in their beds like normal people. If she needed to, she would scream. She would pull the dead out of the ground with her screaming.

'So this is where you hang out at night.' Connor scanned the water, his voice conversational. She wondered if he could see the spirits, if the spirits could see the two humans sitting on the night edge of the lake. If she spoke, maybe she would feel less fear.

'Why aren't you doing your camp-fire thing?' she asked slowly.

He was several inches taller, and so close she could smell his shampoo. Plucking a stalk of grass, he began shredding it. 'Just looking for my lost arrows,' he said softly.

'Yeah, well, I found mine,' she said, starting to get up, but he grabbed her wrist.

'C'mon.' Suddenly his face was full of smiles. 'I saw you sitting here, so I came over to check out your arm. How's your arm, Adrien?'

'It'd be fine,' she said, 'if you let go of it.'

Letting go of her arm, he started rubbing her shoulder. 'Let's make pax, eh?' he said. 'I don't want to spend my summer fighting with the boss's niece. Erin'll fire me if you don't like me.'

'Stop touching me,' she said.

'Pax?' He slid an arm around her, and she pushed at him.

'Pax or kiss my ass?' she hissed.

He let go of her then. 'Either,' he said coolly.

The lake lapped at their ears; the beach was a calm

93

splash of moonlight. For an odd moment, his eyes lingered on her mouth.

Her heart pounded. 'Neither,' she said harshly.

For a moment they remained frozen, staring at each other, and then Connor jumped off the ridge, taking the steep drop to the sand and landing on his feet.

'This is neither,' he said. 'I'll take you midnight canoeing.'

'Isn't that against the rules?'

'They're my rules,' he grinned. 'I'm in charge of the waterfront. I won't tell, you won't tell. It'll be our secret.'

She hesitated, and he stepped closer. 'Listen,' he said, his voice hoarse, his face almost frightened. 'It was a joke, okay? I didn't mean to hit you with that arrow, I swear.'

'Well, you did.'

'I'm sorry,' he said. 'Look, I apologize. It was a dumb, stupid, dork-brain thing to do.'

He stood in front of her, one hand outstretched – tall, broad-shouldered, probably twenty-one. It was a moment to take hold of, a moment that could change things. Any one of the five girls from Prairie Sky would have jumped at the chance. Briefly Adrien wavered. Maybe she was over-reacting, she thought. Like he said, it was nothing more than a joke gone wrong. She hadn't died, after all. And everyone made mistakes, didn't they? Here was an opportunity to make pax, go night canoeing and come back different, laughing and carefree like a popular girl. She would be popular if Connor liked her, she would have friends . . .

Out on the water the spirits were rising, their arms reaching towards her, their mouths opening in a low wail. Their sound twisted through her; every fibre in her body vibrated with the long, thin moans of the dead girls on the lake.

'Maybe not tonight,' she said uncertainly, watching them. 'I'm tired.'

'You're not scared of a little water, are you?' Stepping closer, Connor looked up at her. 'Is it your aunt you're worried about? I can handle her.'

Abruptly she remembered the stamp-grunt combo. As her head cleared, she couldn't believe she had been about to get in a canoe with this jerk. 'You're lucky she doesn't know about your camp-fire shit,' she said haughtily.

'Oh, she knows,' Connor said. 'The sweet boss knows all right.'

In spite of what Paul had told her, Adrien couldn't believe her aunt would ever have sneaked out to any middle-of-the-night camp-fires, even twenty years ago. Giving a scornful laugh, she said, 'She'd fire you so fast.'

Still smiling, Connor raised his hands. 'It's a tradition,' he said. 'Hey, it's been around longer than she has. Goes back as long as Camp Lakeshore.' He took a step forward. 'What d'you think your precious auntie did at night when she first started working here?'

'Not that,' snapped Adrien. Wild fury rose in her. 'She was a counsellor, not skills or maintenance. She had kids to take care of, she would've been responsible.'

Slowly, easily, Connor started to laugh.

'Stop laughing,' Adrien demanded. 'And stop talking about her like that.'

With a smooth gesture, Connor passed a hand over his face, wiping the laughter clean. For a moment he stood motionless and gorgeous in the moonlight, then took a sudden run up the path and jogged across the lawn towards the trees. 'Beer calls,' he waved. 'Ta-ta . . .'

Bewildered, she turned back to the spirits. At some point in the conversation they had stopped wailing and were now floating on the quiet water, their bodies intertwined as if they were extensions of one another. Adrien wasn't certain, but she thought they were watching her. Closer than a mother, closer than a father. Closer than any aunt. The spirits watched her the way she watched them.

'I love you,' she whispered to the five dead girls. Then she turned, heading across the lawn to her empty cabin, the loneliness that would not leave her, and deep, dreaming sleep.

Seven

Saturday morning, Adrien sat on the office steps and watched joking groups of staff climb into cars and drive away. Dressed in shorts and swimsuits, they carried hats and sunscreen, and were headed for a nearby public beach. Usually, she could count on receiving at least a few calls of 'Hey Grouch, how's the swamp?' but today no one waved or spoke to her. After last night's chat on the beach, Connor must have told everyone at the camp-fire to give her the cold shoulder for refusing pax. She felt invisible, part of another dimension. When she saw Darcie approaching, arm-in-arm with Connor, laughing and bumping hips, Adrien retreated into the office and watched from a window as they climbed into Connor's Toyota. Several others joined them, but her stomach still felt like the bottom of a lake. So much for her roommate's promise of eternal friendship.

Spitting gravel, the Toyota drove off, and Adrien returned to the porch steps. As the last cars left, a rustling quiet descended onto the grounds. Birds called back and forth. Far off, the lake glinted. Glumly Adrien plucked off a few mayflies and picked at a mosquito bite. A faint buzz could be heard coming down the road, a single vehicle travelling into the grounds, and she hazarded a guess at who it might be – a member of staff who had forgotten sunscreen?

She thought about staking out Prairie Sky, spying on the girls who had stayed there twenty years ago. But was it spying? she wondered guiltily. She hadn't gone looking for them, and she hadn't asked to see their spirits. It was almost as if they were showing themselves to her. Some time last night, she had woken to find herself sleeping in a cabin full of girls her own age. She had been lying in an upper bunk, and the sound of the other girls' deep sleep-breathing had risen towards her, rocking her like a cradle. *Not alone*, she had thought. *Not alone.* For a brief moment, she and the girls had dreamed together – something about water, endless, gentle water. Then she had woken a second time to see Darcie's empty bed, and the only sounds in the cabin had been her own.

With a loud rumble, a dirt bike pulled onto the walkway in front of her and stopped. A helmet hid the rider's face, but she recognized his butt. Leaning forward, Paul cut the engine. 'Want a ride?' he asked.

Adrien was caught in the sudden wild beating of her heart. 'A ride where?' she said guardedly.

Unstrapping a second helmet from the handlebars, he handed it to her. 'You ever been dirt biking?'

'No.' Stunned, she stared at the helmet in her hands. She had thought this day would belong to the usual loneliness, but unexpectedly it was changing shape, new places opening in the air, in her mind. Slowly she put on the helmet.

'Leave a note for Erin,' said Paul.

'Why?'

'You're her niece. It's genetic — she'll worry.'

Adrien had never even *thought* about being on a dirt bike. Her mother got fidgety if she looked at a twelve-speed. Cautiously, she got on behind Paul. She tried to leave some room, but the angle of the seat slid her up against his butt. They were plastered together.

'Use the footrests,' Paul hollered as the engine roared to life. 'And hang on. I'm your seatbelt.'

Adrien hesitated. This was starting to feel like a massage parlour. Then Paul gunned the bike, it jumped forward, and she had to grab something to stay on. By the time her head cleared, they were passing the corrals, and her arms were wrapped around him in a death grip. *How embarrassing*, she thought, flustered. But this was nothing like being in a car — the ground went by at an alarming speed, and it looked so close. Instinctively, her arms tightened. Emerging from the wooded area, Paul stopped at the edge of the grounds, where the camp road connected to a highway. A few cars whizzed by.

'You all right?' he asked.

'Yeah,' she said to the back of his helmet.

'Don't let go,' he said, and turned onto a well-worn dirt path that ran parallel to the highway. As they zoomed along, the track dipped and swerved through blond grass that rose to her waist and brushed her bare arms. The engine thrummed constantly beneath her, Paul's back shifted warm against her chest. About her, everything was sun, wind and sky. Abruptly they came to a split in the trail and Paul took the path leading away from the highway, across a scrubby field and up a hill. When they crested, he stopped briefly. Ahead lay a series of hills, laced with dirt paths. Several bikes could be seen close by, jetting puffs of dust as they skidded and swerved.

Paul turned his head and spoke sideways. 'Cousins,' he said.

Great, she thought. *A family reunion.* 'You're not going to do that, are you?' she asked, pointing to a bike that was mid-air, coming off a ridge.

'You'll be okay if you keep hanging on like that,' he grinned.

Flushing, Adrien let go, but Paul took her hands and pulled them back around his waist. 'Keep your seatbelt fastened,' he said and revved the engine.

Adrien gave an exasperated snort, but soon lost the irritation. It was difficult to keep up the Grouch act out here. She couldn't stop breathing the warm grass scent, couldn't stop *knowing* she was breathing. Above her head spread a sheer blue sky. It felt like the dome of her brain, as if somehow her skull had lifted off and she had become one with an endless blue, floating above the rippling blond hills. 'It's so pretty out here,' she said.

'Yeah,' said Paul, 'it is.'

A shout came from below as the other bikers caught sight of them. Sticking two fingers into his mouth, Paul gave an ear-splitting whistle. Ear-splitting whistles replied.

'Found your wings yet, Angel?' he asked.

'Adrien,' she said automatically, still watching the sky.

'Well, Adrien.' Paul leaned forward, pulling her with him. 'Let's fly.'

With a spurt, the bike careened downward, leaving her scream behind them at the crest of the hill. The next hour was a blurred weave of beige grass and brown earth, following paths that rose towards sky, then descended again. She soon felt it, a liquid, ceaseless flight that could have been a fantasy of riding the wind but for the sound of the engine and the feel of Paul's body pulling her into the next swerve of the bike. After a while she lost even this and became only motion, riding earth, cresting sky, catching the sun in her mouth and letting it out again into the endless blue. When Paul finally cut the engine, the silence was shattering. She pulled off her helmet, and her ears vibrated with the quiet As she slid off the bike, every part of her body ached: her arms, the inside of her legs, even her butt. Gradually sound returned and she could hear the wind sighing in the grass, the distant whine of the other bikes. Paul spoke, his voice so complete it seemed to rise out of the earth.

'How'd you like it?' He stood beside her, running his hands through his sweaty hair. The usual heaviness that sat on him was gone, as if he had dumped his sixth sense for the day and was living inside the other five.

Adrien breathed the deep, warm scent of grass and

earth. 'I want my own bike,' she said. 'I want my own bunch of hills. And I want this sky.'

He grinned. 'You want a smoke?'

'Yeah,' she said. '*And* lunch. *And* a bathroom.'

He pointed to a large rock with a small shadow, the only privacy the area offered. As Adrien squatted, her knees creaked and the ground still seemed to be moving, but desperation made do. When she returned, Paul was sitting on the ground, talking to one of his cousins. The other bikers were a crest of noise, cruising towards them.

'So who's your girlfriend?' asked the skinny, nervous-looking cousin, obviously well known for his tact.

'Adrien,' said Paul, handing her a pack of cigarettes. 'She works at Camp Lakeshore. Adrien, this is Rene.'

Rene had obviously mastered the art of checking out a girl with his peripheral vision. Giving her a sideways grin, he asked, 'So you like biking?'

'Paul's giving me his bike,' Adrien said immediately. 'At the end of the day it's staying with me and he's walking home.'

Paul laughed softly.

'Engaged already,' said Rene, giving Paul's shoulder a congratulatory pat. Again flustered, Adrien concentrated on lighting a cigarette as the other cousins pulled off their helmets and were introduced: Claude, Philippe, and Bette, a burly, short-haired redhead who could be taken for a boy at a glance. As they talked about an upcoming rodeo, Adrien sat stripping grass and watching from her usual position outside the conversation. Except that this time the earth vibrated beneath her like the roar of a bike, and her blood was madly cruising every artery. Then her stomach let loose with a loud grumble and she stood.

'I need food,' she said to Paul.

'Yup, me too.' He pulled on his helmet. 'See you guys.'

'Invite us to the wedding,' Rene called as they got onto the bike. Adrien grunted slightly as her body settled back into its worst aches. With a wave, Paul swung the bike onto the track. Now that she had been called his girlfriend, Adrien thought, holding onto him was different. When they touched, her skin felt warm and sweet. Why hadn't Paul told Rene they just shared smokes and talked?

'Where are we going?' she yelled at his helmet.

'Food,' he yelled back. A short while later, they pulled up in front of a farmhouse and Paul cut the engine. In the sudden quiet, Adrien tried but couldn't move. The slightest shift was torture.

'Stiff?' Sliding awkwardly off the front of the seat, Paul turned to help her.

'Rigor mortis,' she groaned.

He gave a soft grin. His eyes were like moss, velvety. 'Hold still,' he said, undid her helmet and took it off. Then he reached into her hair and gently removed something – a mayfly, its pale wings slightly mangled, but alive. 'Hitched a ride,' said Paul. They watched it wobble off his hand, flutter a short distance, and disappear into the grass.

'Won't last long,' said Adrien.

'Who does?' asked Paul.

'I'm glad I lasted longer than two days,' she said.

'Two days is eighty years to them,' said Paul. 'Imagine what it'd be like if life was just water and grass and sky. Heaven, don't you think?'

'Earth,' said Adrien. 'What kind of life is it to live at the bottom of a lake for two years, so you can fly for two days, spawn, and die?'

'I like the middle part,' he said. 'I bet they make every second count.'

Adrien had never felt so much heat. Concentrating furiously, she lugged her aching body off the bike, just as a small girl in overalls and braids came running up, an ageing collie loping along behind her.

'Who's she?' demanded the girl.

'She is Adrien, Michelle,' said Paul.

'Why is her face so red?' asked Michelle.

The red deepened. Desperately, Adrien wished for the Big One.

'Windburn,' said Paul. He touched her arm, and Adrien managed a sideways glance. 'C'mon in for lunch,' he added.

They headed for the front porch, Michelle trailing behind. 'She's your girlfriend,' the little girl announced, 'because Leanne dumped you, and now you don't got one.'

Something shot through Adrien, hot and painful.

'Leanne moved to Regina,' Paul said stiffly. 'And we were just friends.'

'I saw you kissing her,' Michelle insisted shrilly.

Taking a deep breath, Paul glanced at Adrien. 'How stiff are you?' he asked. 'Need help climbing the stairs?'

She looked away. 'I'll be all right.'

'Hope you're hungry.' He took the steps in a single bound. 'We've got loads of food.'

Food turned out to mean everything from baked beans to leftover lasagna to angel food cake, with a few sardines thrown in for dessert. As they ate, Paul's mother hovered about the kitchen, wearing overalls and braids like her daughter, constant movement and chatter. She watched Adrien, and Adrien watched her.

'Now, Michelle,' said Mrs Marchand, 'you've already had your lunch, and you had two pieces of cake, and why are you wearing your shoes in the kitchen? Take this out to Sheltee, she's losing too much weight. Adrien, Paul tells me you're Erin Wood's niece. She's been a good solid camp director all these years, don't you think? This is the day I always think of it, all those young ones packing their suitcases and sleeping bags for their first week at camp. I remember when your city cousin Annette used to go, Paul. Always wanted to take half the house. Couldn't fit it all –'

Without warning, the window curtains gusted sharply, and the air changed. City air, thought Adrien, breathing it in. It was easy to smell the difference. As she watched from her seat at the table, the Marchands' kitchen walls darkened to burgundy-blue, Paul and his mother faded, and then a different room came into view – a bedroom that looked normal but felt too intense, like breathing in a dream. The door opened and a girl walked in, set a suitcase onto the bed, and opened it. Startled, Adrien realized it was one of the girls from the photograph, the one who laughed the loudest, the one she would have chosen first as a friend. Pulling out a dresser drawer, the girl started chucking underwear and socks into the suitcase as if it was a basketball hoop.

'Roberta,' called a voice, and a look-alike woman appeared in the doorway, carrying a load of folded laundry. 'Seven pairs of socks and seven pairs of under-wear,' she admonished. 'Last year you took twice as many and lost most of them.'

'The guys do panty raids, Mom,' Roberta protested. 'I need extra, or I won't have any left.'

'Seven of each,' her mother said firmly. 'Your jeans are in the dryer.' She went out again.

With a scowl Roberta turned towards the suitcase and muttered, 'How can I help it if my panties are pop-ular?' Dramatically she counted out seven pairs of socks and underwear, and tossed the rest onto the floor. Then she began to pack the laundry her mother had brought in, humming quietly to herself – an old tune about a bullfrog named Jeremiah who liked to share wine.

At that moment something else drifted into the bed-room, a human shape twisting in a grey, smoky haze – one of the five spirits from the lake. Oblivious, the girl continued to hum and pack, not noticing as the spirit tucked extra articles into the suitcase: a skull, a femur, part of a pelvis. Spirit bones, they shimmered with a grey glow, and Roberta's hands passed directly through them as she folded, patted, and counted. She and the spirit looked so comfortable together, thought Adrien in astonishment, the spirit weaving itself in a caress about the humming girl as if it was nothing more than the lilt of her voice.

Then it turned, and Adrien felt the spirit look directly at her, as if it knew she was watching, as if it had brought this moment to her and laid it open in her mind like a gift.

Abruptly she was back in the Marchands' kitchen. The radio was tuned to a golden oldies station, Three Dog Night were singing 'Joy to the World', and Mrs Marchand was still talking as Michelle called to her from outside.

'What could that girl want now?' Mrs Marchand sighed, going out of the door.

'Adrien?' said Paul. Leaned forward, he was watching her closely. 'Where the hell are you?'

She stared at him, her eyes straining to return to the bedroom where a girl and her spirit packed life and death into the same suitcase.

'I –' she stammered. 'I just had a daydream, but it was so real. I saw a girl Aunt Erin counselled twenty years ago. She's one of the ghosts from Prairie Sky. She wasn't dead yet, she was getting ready to come to camp – packing, like your mom said camp kids would be doing today. In my daydream the girl's spirit was beside her, outside her body, like she was both dead and alive at the same time, and it was packing bones into her suitcase. She must've died while she was at camp. I bet you that's what it means. I bet you Aunt Erin had five campers who all died at Camp Lakeshore while she was their counsellor. That's why Prairie Sky is haunted. That's why their spirits are on the lake.'

Paul let out a slow whoosh of air. 'So you did see ghosts in Prairie Sky.'

'I've been seeing them all over the camp,' Adrien muttered. 'Almost from the minute I got there. Don't you see them?'

He shook his head. 'I just feel something. The dead don't talk to me.'

'They're not talking to me,' said Adrien, 'just . . . showing me things. Their lives.' Her eyes hung onto his face. 'I feel like they've got something to tell me.'

'But they're dead,' he said intensely. 'Why would the dead want to talk to you?'

'They don't feel dead,' she said. 'They feel . . . like me.'

'They don't creep you out?' he asked.

'Do I creep you out?' she said.

'You're not dead,' he said.

'Yet,' she said.

He went as still as caught breath, and she watched thoughts pass through his face. Finally he nodded, as if they had come to an agreement and the understanding between them was complete.

'Yet,' he said softly, 'that's what we've got – you and me.'

That afternoon they rode for hours, just the two of them, past fields of wheat and rapeseed, farmhouses and barking dogs – a world they passed through, but were no longer part of. They knew now, accepted that they had been set aside, chosen for a mystery that was fast approaching. They could ignore it, try to hide from it, or ride towards it in a thin, grim line, seeking its face. All afternoon, they rode seeking. After a while they removed their helmets, Paul strapped them to the bike, and they rode full into the wind, Adrien resting her face against his back while her hair flew free. She no longer thought about holding onto him – they had become part of sun, sky, and wind. For hours that afternoon, they did not touch ground. They lifted above the sound of the bike and flew in their wild, seeking heartbeats, until it was time to return to earth again.

As Paul turned onto the Camp Lakeshore road, Adrien came back to herself, the stiff ache of her body, the warm sweat of his back. Paul's back, she realized suddenly. She was all over him. Immediately she tried to straighten up, but the ache in her muscles let loose with pure fire. When he stopped a short way up the road, out of sight of the office, she dragged herself off the bike and stood holding her back in disbelief.

'It'll wear off,' said Paul, his voice cracking after its afternoon of silence.

'How long am I going to feel like this?' she groaned.

Before she could move, he was holding her. All the warmth in the world stepped close and wrapped its arms around her, Paul's face in her tangled hair, his breathing in her neck. A wild longing came through her; she saw herself doing things she had never imagined. Slowly, she put her arms around him, let herself touch his sweaty back. He was trembling.

'Sometimes it's fire,' he said softly. 'I can smell my skin burning. Or it's drowning, and I'm begging for air. Lots of times, it's falling. I'm caught in an endless fall, and I never know when I'm gonna crash.'

'What day is it?' she asked hoarsely. 'What day are you supposed to die?'

'My birthday,' he said. His arms tightened and a gust of sound came out of him. 'God, I want to live.'

Pulling free, he turned quickly, mounted his bike, and rode off. Surrounded by the scent and whisper of trees, she watched the late-afternoon sun touch long golden fingers to what looked like the beginning of wings on his back, fragile and iridescent as a mayfly's.

Adrien found her aunt in Prairie Sky, sitting on one of the bottom bunks. As she stepped through the doorway, she glanced around, trying to see it for the first time as Roberta would have. Who would she be looking at? Adrien wondered. Nat? The girl with the red ponytail?

At that moment the cabin wavered slightly and someone took shape, turning towards Adrien – a young woman with a tall, proud face, blonde straight-falling hair, the palest blue eyes. Twenty years ago, Erin Wood had carried the world like a scenic backdrop. Anyone seeing her for the first time would have been mesmerized – Roberta, that entire cabin of girls. Astounded, Adrien blinked, the young Erin Wood vanished, and her thirty-eight-year-old aunt came into view, lines drawn deeply about the mouth and eyes, but the shoulders holding firm.

'Aunt Erin,' said Adrien. She walked towards her aunt, the evening deepening about her, secret worlds watching from the other side of consciousness. 'I want to give this back.' Carefully she held out the photograph, a moment from the past that held so many meanings. As her aunt caught sight of it, her shoulders slumped and her mouth sucked in. She took it gently, careful not to touch the centre and stain what was left of that twenty-year-old laughter.

'I found it in the office,' Adrien said. 'I'm sorry I didn't give it to you when you asked.'

'Why didn't you?' asked her aunt, staring at the past.

'There was something I didn't understand then,' said Adrien.

'And what is that?'

'You called me here,' said Adrien, pointing to the photograph. 'And so did those girls.'

Their eyes caught, Aunt Erin's mouth coming open in a question she couldn't ask. In response, a surge of strength came through Adrien, causing her to feel strong and solid. At the same time, she was hazy and insubstantial as smoke, the Big One hidden and waiting in the core of her brain.

'Whatever happens,' Adrien said slowly, 'this summer is mine.'

She took a deep breath, tasting the scent of spruce. Then she turned and stepped through the doorway, out into the late green evening, leaving her aunt alone in the cabin, holding onto something no one else understood.

Part II

Eight

The first camper arrived at ten fifty-two a.m., carrying a small ghetto-blaster and dragging a pair of exhausted-looking parents. Aunt Erin moved in quickly, taking out a list marked *Campers' Rules* and reminding the parents of rule number eight: no radios or ghetto-blasters of any kind. Then she suggested the family tour the grounds and acquaint themselves with the facilities – refreshments could be purchased at Tuck-'n'-Tack. Adrien sold them one package of Nibs, two Malted Milks, three Sprites and an ugly blue sweatshirt, size small.

'Haven't you got any better colours?' demanded the nine-year-old camper, pushing her glasses up her nose and glaring at the T-shirts in the display case. Adrien liked her immediately.

'The person in charge of T-shirt colours', she said, pointing, 'is that lady over there.'

'The one who won't let me keep my ghetto-blaster?' asked the girl.

'That's the one.'

'You look like her.'

'Impossible,' said Adrien. 'I think those T-shirts are extremely ugly too.'

The girl's grin was full of crooked teeth. The next time Adrien looked up, she saw her aunt receiving an earful about colours from a skinny squirt whose arms were crossed authoritatively over her chest. She would have savoured the moment, but the grounds were rapidly filling with campers and their families, and she was kept busy selling candy, T-shirts, buttons, postcards, calendars and datebooks, even nature-sound cassettes. Tuck-'n'-Tack also handled the rental equipment for the mini-golf course and the volleyball court. Adrien had just handed out the last set of clubs and was tearing open yet another container of Smarties, yelling inside her head for a five-minute break, a cigarette, the Big One, *anything* to get some relief, when she turned to serve the next person in line, and it was Roberta.

The girl was there and not there. Adrien could see her face clearly, but she was transparent as she had been in the cabin, a thin film of the past superimposed over the present tense. So were her parents, who stood in line behind her.

'I'd like a green sweatshirt,' said Roberta. Her dark hair was pulled into a short ponytail and she wore a neon-pink Beatles T-shirt. Released from Aunt Erin's photograph, her face seemed so alive, constantly on the verge of laughter, her left cheek dancing in and out of a dimple. Her only makeup was a beauty mark drawn above her upper lip. Adrien was sure it hadn't been in

116

the photograph. 'What size d'you think, Mom?' Roberta asked, looking over her shoulder.

'Oh, large,' said her mother, smiling the same dimple. 'It'll shrink and God knows, you'll grow.'

'And a Big Turk,' Roberta said, turning back. 'And a Mountain Dew. What d'you want, Shrimp?'

'I'm not a shrimp,' insisted a short, small voice. Leaning forward, Adrien caught sight of a four-year-old boy busily punching his older sister's leg.

'Dad, tell the jerk to stop punching me,' Roberta said.

'Stop calling him names then,' said her father wearily.

Another transparent family walked up behind Roberta's, and a girl with a long red ponytail leaned on the counter. 'Got any Jaw Breakers?' she asked.

This girl was slightly taller than Roberta. Her face was thin, her mouth pouty. She wore heavy green eyeshadow, a familiar striped tube top, and a ring with a large stone. The two girls gave each other sideways glances while Adrien stared.

'Sherry, could you ask about T-shirts?' asked a plump, red-haired woman in a flower-power dress left over from the 1960s. Her makeup left Sherry's in the dust. 'For your cousin Billy's birthday, remember?'

Giving her ponytail a scornful flip, Sherry said, 'Yeah, Mom, I'm not stupid.'

'I didn't say you were stupid,' snapped her mother in exasperation. 'And I hope this week at camp teaches you some manners. When will you learn to respect your el—'

Roberta shot Sherry a sympathetic grin, and the two

girls tuned the adults out. 'I like your mood stone,' she said. 'Mom made me leave mine at home.'

They shared eye-rolling until a mayfly landed on Sherry's bare shoulder. 'Ugh,' she cried, pulling it off.

'Those were here last year too,' said Roberta. 'They stick to you like glue, but they don't bite. They only last for a week or so, and then they're gone. What cabin are you in?'

'Some dork name,' said Sherry. 'Prairie . . . something or other.'

'Sky,' said Roberta.

'More like Prairie Yawn,' said Sherry. 'This place is for the dead.'

'We'll wake it up,' said Roberta. 'Hey, get a T-shirt if you can.'

'They're so ugly,' complained Sherry. 'Boats?!'

'We'll decorate them,' grinned Roberta. 'Tie-dye in Farts and Crafts.' She blew a mouth fart on her arm.

'Roberta, would you hurry it up?' said her father.

'See ya later, eh?' said Sherry.

'Yeah, see ya,' grinned Roberta.

With that the girls vanished, and Adrien found herself staring into the eye sockets of a skull on a very tall T-shirt. 'Gimme a blue sweatshirt,' said the living face above the skull. 'And a Mr Big.'

Even though she knew they were gone, Adrien couldn't help leaning over the counter and scanning for the girls. Around the office, crowds of people were coming and going, or chattering in small groups. Small children ran past in frantic bursts of energy, and a few teenagers were punting a ball back and forth over the volleyball net. Suddenly Adrien felt very cold. This was how the camp must have looked to Roberta and Sherry on their arrival day twenty years ago, she realized: Camp Lakeshore T-shirts everywhere, children zooming around. Not the slightest sign of death.

'What're you staring at?' demanded the boy wearing the skull. 'The sweatshirts are behind you, *duh.*' Pulling a mayfly off his neck, he held it by the wings. 'What are these creepy things?'

'They're called mayflies,' said Adrien, handing him a sweatshirt. 'They're like large mosquitoes. They take a huge chunk out of you when they bite. Worse than horseflies.'

With a yelp, the boy swiped several more off his arms.

'You owe me twenty-seven dollars and ninety-four cents,' she smiled, keying it into the till. 'I hope you enjoy wearing your Camp Lakeshore sweatshirt. Those boats will look lovely on you.'

Adrien was closing the awning, about to head into the dining hall for lunch, when Paul coasted up on a ten-speed. Immediately an intense flush started crawling up her neck and she kicked at the wall, concentrating on the pain in her foot. 'Where's your dirt bike?' she asked loudly.

'Come up to the corrals with me?' he asked, ignoring her question. From the look on his face, Adrien thought, dismayed, yesterday hadn't happened; they hadn't spent hours riding the wind in that long, raw closeness.

'Sure,' she said faintly, closing the padlock. 'I just have to take the till into the office.'

They rode double to the corrals, Adrien leaning backwards and swearing never to touch him again, but when they arrived she immediately forgot about it. 'How did this happen?' she cried, running to a broken section in the fence.

'I dunno.' Removing his baseball cap, Paul ran a hand through his flattened hair. 'It was like this when I got here. It took me over an hour to get the horses back in. They were wandering all over the woods. I just fixed this section three days ago.'

'Would the horses knock it down?' asked Adrien, squatting to look more closely. Several rails had been dislodged. The nails had come out clean.

'No,' he said shortly. 'They scratch themselves against the fence but they don't take runs at it. Those rails weren't loose, unless I didn't nail them in properly.'

The large paddock stretched back into a swampy wooded area. 'Did you check over there?' she asked, pointing.

'I checked all of it,' he said. 'This is the only part that gave.'

'I don't think it was you, Paul,' she said, recalling the staff orienteering exercise from the first day of Training Session. How many groups had seen Paul fixing this section?

'Neither do I,' he said quietly. 'But who could it be? And why?'

He gave her a hand up and she stood. When she looked into his face this time, yesterday was there, warm and intense. For a second she wanted to stub her toe again, find some way out of what she was feeling. Everything got so *hot*.

'Adrien,' he murmured. No one had ever said her name like that, she thought – softly, as if touching it. Paul's face was also flushed. His eyes flicked away, then back, and she realized he was feeling the same confusion. 'I dreamt about you last night,' he said.

'Did you die?' she asked quickly.

'I heard you calling my name,' he said, 'and I woke up. You saved me.'

'Good,' she burst out, sudden tears in her eyes. 'I saw those girls this morning, while I was working in Tuck-'n'-Tack. They're here now. They're at camp and they're going to die. I don't want you to die too. Please stop dreaming those dreams.'

'I can't stop dreaming,' he said. 'I dream all night. I wake up covered in sweat. I'm tired, like I haven't slept.'

'Then I'm going to be in all your dreams,' she said fiercely. 'And I'm going to stop you from dying in every one of them.'

Smiling slightly, he touched her cheek, and she burned a long slow fire. 'I feel so many things,' he said, his eyes searching her face as if she was the last living thing. 'A minute's like a year rushing past. Everything's so vivid. I've been dreaming about you for two years, and now you're here.'

Tears ran down her face. She didn't know what he

was telling her. 'Your birthday?' she asked. 'Is it this week?'

'Soon,' he said.

'Why won't you tell me the day?'

'If you don't know,' he said intensely, 'it might not happen.'

'You really think I can change things?'

The wind was everywhere, touching the leaves, the grass, her skin. She knew if she could do this, she could do anything, be anyone. Slowly she reached out and traced the soft flush of his lower lip. It was like touching a dream, except it was real – she could feel the gentle give of his lip, its slight wetness. Paul closed his eyes, his breathing deepening.

'Adrien,' he said. 'Adrien, listen, okay?' Opening his eyes, he caught her hand and held it. 'D'you remember yesterday, when my sister Michelle was talking about Leanne? Well, she was right. Leanne did dump me.'

Startled, Adrien stood trapped by this change in conversation. She didn't want to hear about Leanne, she wanted to step back into her dream of touching his mouth, listening to him breathe deeper and deeper into himself.

'This is hard,' Paul said hoarsely. 'I've never told anyone about this, okay?'

Abruptly she woke to the fear in his eyes. A hole opened in her gut, but she nodded. He let go of her hand.

'I hurt her,' he said quickly. 'I didn't know it'd turn out like that, I swear. It's just – I get crazy, all this shit coming at me in my head. You don't know what I'm like in here.' Hissing, he hit his forehead with the heel of his hand. 'Thinking about dying all the time, all the different ways. Thinking about missing the rest of my life. It makes me crazy to have everything now. Everything *now*,' he said bitterly. 'Mostly I hold it in, but Leanne and I were close, friends since grade four. We weren't really going out, I guess I talked her into it. She didn't really want to, I knew that.' He stared off, his mouth working. 'Afterwards, she wouldn't talk to me. She never talked to me again. I wrecked something for her, something important – a lot more important than what I got out of it, that's for sure.' He rubbed at a trembling in his mouth, then chanced a glance at Adrien. 'I'm a shit, right?'

'You're not a shit,' said Adrien. 'And I'm not Leanne.'

Sighing, Paul slumped against the fence. 'Two years I've been dreaming about you,' he said.

'It's been two years since I had my aneurysm,' Adrien said slowly.

'Must mean something,' he muttered. 'How're you supposed to know? I don't have a fucking clue what I'm supposed to do, how I'm supposed to be. Is there some purpose to all this? Y'know, like this is the way I'm finally gonna wise up and become a better person. Well, if it is, I already learned, okay? I know what an absolute jerk I can be, so until this is all over – whatever that means – everything's on hold. I'm on hold. Life is on hold.'

'But –' said Adrien. Out in the corrals, horses whickered

and nuzzled. Horses had it so easy, she thought. They didn't have to talk about it, they just did it. Words were an impossible dream. 'Shit!' she erupted. 'I wish I was a horse.'

Paul followed her gaze out into the paddock, just as one horse began nosing the rump of another.

'Not that horse,' she said desperately.

Paul gave a shout of laughter and pulled his baseball cap back on. 'The day after my birthday,' he said, 'if I'm still around, I am going into those trees. And if you come after me, we are going to build a lean-to, crawl into it, and not come out for a long time.'

'Why not now?' asked Adrien in a small, hopeful voice.

'I'm still a crazy dying shit,' Paul said simply.

It was five fifteen, the dining hall a mass of shouting, fidgeting children. As the serving line moved slowly along the counter, the hairnets were dumping large helpings of chilli, corn and coleslaw onto pale yellow plates. Slinking in through a side entrance, Adrien joined the closest staff table. Big mistake, she realized immediately. This table had got through the serving line early, and were already half-way through the mess on their plates. Earlier that day, she had missed lunch because she had stayed at the corrals to help Paul with the fence. The hairnets had given them a few sandwiches, but now she was absolutely starved. She couldn't remember being this hungry as a camper. Buttering a slice of bread, she wolfed it down.

'So,' said a voice. 'How's little Wood?'

Glancing across the table, she saw Connor mopping up the last of his sloppy joes with a piece of bread. That afternoon he had been at the docks, putting groups of cabins through their waterfront orientation. Tuck-'n'-Tack was closed on Sunday afternoons, so after the fence had been fixed Adrien had worked at the office computer, helping Gwen slot cabins into a master activities schedule. From there she had watched groups of children sitting on the lawn, waiting to get their medical records checked at the first-aid cabin. Beyond them, Connor had stridden up and down the horizon like a bronze god, blond halo gleaming as he explained life-jacket fastenings and how to hold onto a tipped canoe.

'Busy,' Adrien replied tersely.

'Now, what could keep a little girl like you busy?' he drawled, leaning back and patting his stomach.

'Fixing the fence up at the corrals,' she said. 'Someone vandalized it.'

His eyebrows made a careful ascent. *Manufactured shock*, Adrien thought. *He's not really surprised*.

'Yeah,' she continued. 'It must've happened last night. Late last night. Y'know, some stupid drunks thought they'd have a good time letting out the horses.'

'Sounds like the way I'd want to spend a good drunk,' Connor said sarcastically.

Ignoring this, she plunged on. 'But of course, they were too drunk to unhitch the gate. Oh no, they had to take the fence apart.'

'Probably some of the natives,' he said easily. 'Paul and his buddies.'

'I don't think so!' she hissed. 'More like initiation for new recruits, don't you think?'

Up and down the table, staff members had fallen completely silent. Among the shouts and laughter of several hundred children, it was an odd oasis of quiet. Hand shaking, Adrien reached for the bread basket, but Connor pulled it out of reach.

'Uh-uh,' he said, smiling coldly. 'Tsk-tsk.'

'I don't have to play your stupid games,' she said, enunciating clearly. 'Midnight fire. Good times. The training manual is trash.'

Instantly the member of staff sitting next to Connor froze with her fork in her mouth. Even Connor had gone very still. Then a throat at the other end of the table cleared itself loudly and said, 'Con, pass me that bread, would ya?'

'Sure, Bunter,' said Connor. 'Catch.' He tossed the basket and the other guy caught it neatly, removing the last few pieces of bread.

'Sure am hungry,' said Bunter, biting into all three at once.

At that moment Adrien noticed an empty seat at another staff table. She stood, about to walk over to it, but Connor reached across the table and caught her wrist. 'Catch ya later,' he said softly, tightening his grip before letting go.

After supper, everyone filed out of the dining hall to stand in a large circle facing the flagpole. Aunt Erin, remembered Adrien, was a stickler for instilling national pride – twice a day, every day, the entire camp lined up to watch as the flag was raised or lowered. Most of the ceremony took place in complete silence, with only the flag speaking into the wind. Already a camper had been selected to help Aunt Erin fold the flag – the nine-year-old squirt who had lost her ghetto-blaster. Looking ridiculously serious, she stood ramrod-straight at the centre of the circle. It was obvious she had already fallen hopelessly under the camp director's spell. Adrien could almost hear her fierce little heart beat quicker as Aunt Erin stepped forward and began a short speech.

'Tomorrow,' she said slowly and clearly, 'is Canada Day, a day we have set aside to honour our country and celebrate the fact that we live in a place of freedom and dignity.'

Surprised, Adrien focused in on her aunt. She had forgotten the woman could speak in long sentences. 'This flag,' continued Aunt Erin, 'represents what we feel about our country and about ourselves. It stands for everything we believe in: freedom of speech, freedom to worship . . .'

Without warning, Adrien saw five girls step out of the watching crowd and close in on the flagpole. Overhead, the sky had changed, and it seemed to be early morning, the horizon lit with first light. At the top of the flagpole flew a single pair of girl's panties.

'I told Mom!' wailed Roberta. 'They stole all of them. That's the only pair I have left and they stuck it up there.' Hands on hips, she stared up at it, looking very pleased as her pink panties fluttered in the breeze.

'Bet you they're wearing the rest of them,' observed Sherry.

'No way!' gawked a girl with a long tumble of brown hair standing beside her.

'You don't want them back, Roberta,' advised Nat. 'They'll be stretched way out of shape.' She made a lewd gesture and the girls burst into fidgety laughter.

'What'm I gonna wear?' demanded Roberta.

'Nothing,' grinned Nat. 'None of us will, for the whole week. But don't tell Erin, okay? Only us'll know.'

'No underwear?' said the fifth girl, looking shocked.

'C'mon, Cath,' said Nat, 'this is your big chance to dump those bloomers your mother makes you wear.' Quickly she unzipped her shorts, stepped out of them, removed her panties, and pulled her shorts back on. 'Hooey!' she cried, waving her panties over her head. 'Everyone do it!'

'Someone'll see,' protested Cath, looking around.

'Everyone's asleep,' said Nat. 'Erin's snoring and you know why.' Eagerly she began to dance around the flagpole.

'I dunno,' said Cath but the other girls were following suit, sitting down to tug off their jeans.

'My bum's wet from the dew,' laughed Roberta as she scrambled to her feet.

'You've got a bug on it,' Sherry observed.

Delicately Roberta removed the mayfly, then pulled her jeans back on. 'Yahoo!' she cried. Waving her panties over her head, she joined Nat in the dance around the flagpole. Soon the others joined in, giggling and snorting through a wobbly version of 'O Canada'. Finally Sherry stopped dancing and stood staring upward. Her face held a look of awe.

'Let's put them all up there,' she whispered fiercely.

Back in the present tense, Adrien watched the bright red maple leaf descend in small jerks, sagging as it came out of the wind. Then Aunt Erin and her nine-year-old fan were folding the flag and putting it into its overnight box. Serious faces began singing 'O Canada' as a V of geese flew across the lake. Obediently Adrien mouthed the words, but their meaning escaped her. She simply could not believe what she had just seen. Every summer of her childhood she had stood in line on this lawn, morning and evening, listening to her aunt's speeches, watching the red leaf and believing in its holiness. Now for one vivid moment, she saw six pairs of pink and white panties flying wildly at the top of the flagpole, catching the light as the morning sun rose over the lake.

She would never be the same again.

Nine

She was jerked roughly out of sleep, into the glare of a flashlight. Once again, her blankets were pulled off the bed. This time she backed into the wall, shielding her eyes.

'You've broken a long tradition, Grouch,' said someone. It was Connor, speaking in a deep, unfamiliar voice, but she recognized him. What made him think he could pretend to be a different person at night? she wondered. And why did everyone else pretend along with him? Even Darcie was standing near by in the shadows, ready to jump at his slightest command.

'I don't like your traditions,' she said. 'No one made them the law.'

'They're the law here,' he said and pulled her hand from her face. Blinking, she tried to turn her head. 'Bad girls have to be punished, you know.'

'What're you?' she demanded. 'A bunch of Nazis?'

Connor snapped his fingers and two guys leaned towards her – the waterfront assistant and one of the riding instructors. Grabbing her arms, they pulled her off the bed.

'C'mon,' said Connor, leaving the room. Now on her feet, Adrien was pushed towards the door, then forced along the hall. As they emerged outside she started to yell, and a hand was clamped over her mouth. The flashlight was so close, she could feel its heat on her face.

'Make another sound and it'll get worse,' Connor said quietly.

She fell silent. They weren't really hurting her – if she didn't struggle, they held her quite loosely. Slowly the procession wound its way through the trees, past the dining hall and office, then on towards the corrals until it reached the Petting Zoo, a small fenced-in enclosure that housed two sheep, one goat and several rabbits. Every day, the youngest campers came here to feed and pet the animals. As Connor vaulted the fence, the sheep bleated sleepily and backed away.

'Pass her over,' he said.

The fence was no more than a metre high. Adrien kicked and struggled, but was easily lifted into his waiting arms. As they tightened around her, she smelled the beer on his breath and his chin stubble rubbed her cheek. He carried her effortlessly. Several more figures leapt into the enclosure.

'Darcie, get your ass in here,' Connor ordered.

With assistance, Darcie climbed the fence.

'Open it up,' Connor said.

As Darcie took out a key, someone trained the flashlight on the small cage in one corner of the pen that housed the animals' feed. With a start, Adrien remembered that one of her roommate's additional duties was the Petting Zoo's early morning feeding.

'I don't really think we should –' Darcie began, but Connor cut her off.

'Maybe we'll put you in instead?' he jeered.

Resigned, Darcie unlocked the cage. 'It's too full,' she said. 'Grouch won't fit.'

'So pull out a bale,' said Connor.

Hands pulled out the closest bale of hay.

'Great,' said Connor. 'Lots of room. In you go, Grouch. Sit in the cage where all the bad animals belong.'

She tried to hang onto the doorframe, but they pressed her arms to her sides and shoved her through. The small door closed, the padlock clicked shut, and the staff moved in to circle the cage. She counted eleven shapes shifting nervously in the dark.

'Erin Wood,' Connor said, and everyone stamped and grunted. Crouched in the cage, Adrien waited. 'So, little Wood,' Connor sneered, 'how d'you like your new home?'

She couldn't believe the sniggers. They had to be completely drunk, she thought. Too drunk to see her shaking. 'Oh, I'm really scared,' she said. 'The sheep might tear the cage apart and eat me alive. In the morning, my aunt'll find me and you'll be fired.'

'Then maybe we'd better make sure no one finds you,' said Connor. Crouching down by the cage, he pulled out a cigarette lighter and flicked it on. The small flame cast flickering shadows across the bales.

'What're you doing?' gasped Darcie.

'Shut up.' Connor held the flame under several wisps of hay sticking through the wire mesh. 'You gonna tell your auntie, Grouch?' he asked.

'I didn't say I was going to tell,' Adrien said nervously. 'I said she'd find me in the morning if you left me here all night.'

'Oh, we wouldn't do that,' Connor said soothingly. 'Not *all* night, Grouch.'

The hay caught fire and flames shot inward.

'No!' cried Darcie. Shoving Connor aside, she began stamping out the flames with her shoe. As quickly as the fire had flared, it died. 'What d'you think you're doing?' she hissed at him.

'Just testing your loyalties,' he replied.

'You can't kill people,' Darcie protested. 'That's not part of any camp tradition.'

'No one was going to kill her,' Connor said calmly. 'And you interfered.'

'But –' Darcie stammered.

'We're finished here for tonight,' said Connor. 'Beddy-bye for all good staffies. C'mon, Darcie.' Taking her by the shoulders, he pushed her towards the fence. Then he and the others vaulted it, leaving her standing alone, staring at the wire mesh. From the other side, Connor played the flashlight over her face. Everyone watched her take a deep breath, as if coming awake.

'This is stupid,' Darcie said. 'I've got the key.' Walking to the pen's main gate, she unlocked it and stepped out. 'See ya later, Grouch,' she whispered, then joined the others as they headed towards their cabins. Gradually the rustling of leaves faded. There was the distant snapping of a twig, followed by enormous silence. Adrien's heart beat bright stars across the sky.

'This shit only works if everyone believes it,' she yelled into the looming dark, then slumped against the cage door. She couldn't believe they were actually leaving her here.

'On Canada Day,' she muttered. 'Country of freedom and dignity. Freedom of expression and all that.'

The goat was nibbling her hair. Twisting the loose strands into a tight braid, Adrien tucked it into her collar. She was dressed for bed in her usual T-shirt and panties, and the mosquitoes were swarming. Bales crowded her into the cage door, and the top of her head pushed against the mesh roof. More mesh pressed against her back and bare feet. How could Darcie do this? she thought miserably. Tears stung her eyes and throat. *Some friend. Some Spartan.* Darcie was just like everyone else, kissing Connor's ass. Roberta would never have gone along with this shit. Sherry wouldn't have believed in it. Nat would have told Connor to kiss his own ass. Adrien smiled a little, thinking about it. Or *hers*.

It was so quiet, she thought, staring out into the darkness. Everyone was asleep. Were they planning to leave her here all night? What if the Big One hit? It would serve them right if they found her dead in the morning – explain that one to Aunt Erin. Lifting a bare foot, Adrien kicked against the mesh. With a clatter, it belled out but held firm. She kicked again, the mesh cutting into her skin. 'Ouch,' she muttered. She didn't want to wreck the cage, but they had no *right*. Did they expect her to sit quietly until someone came to let her out? Roberta wouldn't, she decided. Nat would tear the cage apart with her bare hands.

'I want out!' Adrien yelled, banging the mesh with her fist. Bright pain laced her skin, followed by a surge of anger, and she punched the mesh a second time. There was no way she was going to sit here, waiting obediently for Connor's return. 'Let me out!' she yelled again and clambered onto her knees. Head pressed against the roof, she pounded her fist in a regular rhythm. Rage rose in her throat, filled her head, and raw words tore out of her. 'I could die,' she shouted. 'Don't you know I could die? I've got a fucked-up brain. It could explode and I'd die out here all alone. It's not my fault. I didn't ask for a defective brain or weak blood vessels. I didn't ask to eat dirt and shit my pants. I used to be like the rest of you and then my life fell apart. I hate being me. I hate me. Let me out.'

Without warning, Darcie was there in the dark, fumbling with the key, unlocking the cage door, and taking her arm. 'All right, okay, take it easy, would ya?' she hissed. 'I was just waiting until they were gone. Shh, you'll wake your aunt. Jesus, what'd you do to your hand?'

Wearily Adrien crawled out and stood shaking as her roommate shone a small flashlight over her right hand. It was lacerated with small cuts. 'Crap,' Darcie muttered.

135

'I'm so sorry, Grouch. I'm so sorry.' Then, before Adrien could move, Darcie wrapped her in a bear hug. Soft and warm, it was full of beating hearts, something to bring her back from the end of the world, the end of herself. 'Shh,' Darcie whispered, 'shh, shh,' as her hair grew soggy from Adrien's tears. 'That's all right,' Darcie soothed. 'That's okay.'

The goat started chewing Adrien's T-shirt. She kicked at it and the two girls pulled apart, wiping away tears. 'Grouch,' Darcie asked hesitantly, 'you were yelling something . . . about your brain? Dying? What –?'

'I had a brain aneurysm,' Adrien gulped, staring off into the dark. 'Two years ago. If it happens again, I'm gone. I was just lucky the first time.'

'Oh,' said Darcie, turning off the flashlight. 'Your aunt didn't tell me.'

'My aunt,' Adrien said scornfully, 'pretends everything's normal. It's my attitude that's the problem. She probably thinks my attitude caused the first one.'

'I doubt it,' said Darcie. The warmth of her hand closed around Adrien's good one. 'C'mon, Grouch. Let's go home.'

Adrien smiled a little. One week in a cabin, she thought, and her roommate called it home. Everywhere Darcie went, home went too. Darcie was her own home. Dropping Adrien's hand, Darcie unlocked the outer gate, then took her hand again firmly, leading her into the trees like a child.

As they walked, an image began to grow in Adrien's mind – cool, quiet, whispering with hidden meanings.

A place where moonlight touched the earth and rooted, going so deep it became darkness. Two halves that connected to form a whole. Her home. Without speaking she turned, taking Darcie with her, and led her towards the lake.

'Where are we going?' Darcie asked. 'I have to fix your hand. I'm tired, I want –'

'Shh,' said Adrien. They were almost at another clearing and small pale shapes could be seen through the trees. Taking a quick breath, Darcie went quiet. Together they crept closer and watched. There in the clearing, they saw one of the youngest cabins – the seven-year-olds. The girls wore sweatshirts and jackets over their nighties, and were clustered around their counsellor in a small awed group, listening.

'It's older than any of us, even me,' the counsellor was saying. 'It's older than your grandma or your great-grandma. This tree is older than any of the animals or buildings here at Camp Lakeshore.'

'Older than the sea?' asked a girl, pointing in the direction of the lake.

'Almost,' said the counsellor. 'This tree is very very old and it's very very wise.'

'How'd it get so smart?' asked another girl.

'Coz it got struck by lightning. Then you're extra smart,' said a third.

'Then you're extra dead,' said the first.

'Not this tree,' said the counsellor. 'This is the Wishing Tree, and it lives just to hear the wishes of children. D'you think it's going to let some dumb ol' lightning

137

come along and kill it?'

'No,' chorused the girls.

Adrien's throat tightened and she blinked fiercely.

'The Wishing Tree is going to hear all your wishes tonight,' the counsellor continued. 'All you have to do is touch the tree and tell it your most secret wish.'

'Do I have to say it out loud?' asked a small voice.

'This tree is so wise, it can hear the softest thought whispered inside your head,' said the counsellor. 'It can hear what no one else can hear. When you're ready, just put your hand on the trunk and wish like this.' Closing her eyes, she stood for a long poised moment, one hand pressed against the white bark. Then she opened her eyes, smiled and stepped back.

'Did the Wishing Tree hear you?' asked a girl.

'Oh yes,' said the counsellor.

'Good,' the girl said fervently. One by one, each child stepped forward and touched the tree. Most of them imitated their counsellor's pose, but one hugged the tree and another stooped to touch the fallen part. When they were finished, the counsellor had them all join hands.

'Now the Wishing Tree knows your wish,' she said. 'Each leaf on these branches holds someone's wish. The Wishing Tree never forgets a wish. Now your wish is up there among the leaves, blowing in the wind.' Open-mouthed, the girls stood listening to the tree rustle until their counsellor took the nearest girl's hand and led them back to their cabin.

'That's Tamai,' sighed Darcie, watching them go. 'Isn't

138

she neat? She missed staff training, but this is her fourth summer so she doesn't need it. She always counsels the youngest girls.'

'They need her,' Adrien said hoarsely. Stepping into the clearing, she stood looking at the tree. Although the moon was partially covered, the trunk still glowed, a shadowy light with a dark burn slash. Leaves on the fallen half were starting to brown. Part of its life was leaving. Walking to the tree, Adrien placed both hands on the standing half. 'C'mere, Spart,' she said.

She needed to say this out loud, and she needed someone to hear it. Quietly Darcie stepped close, her sleeve brushing Adrien's bare arm. For a moment, the Wishing Tree seemed to pause. Its leaves stopped rustling and the air held silent, waiting.

'I want,' Adrien said softly, 'to know about death. How long it takes for the heart to stop beating. When do you stop knowing? What happens when you lose yourself? Does all the light shooting through your brain go out quick like a bedroom light, or does it unravel slow, like a sweater, giving you time? Does the throat clutch up? Can you get out that last important word? How cold will my skin feel? Will I feel it turning cold, or will I already be gone? Will my eyes turn blue? How blue? Will I see only blue things then, only sky? I want to know if you rise up and blow with the wind, or if you sink down, far down into cold water, nothing closes over your face, nothing is all you are, all you ever were.'

Kneeling, she touched the dying half. 'And I want to

know about life,' she added carefully. 'What it's like to truly believe in it. Because life only works if you believe in it, right, Spart?'

'Right,' whispered Darcie.

'So I want to believe in it,' said Adrien, waiting, and the cool green sensation came through her, washing her clean. Breathing deeply, she stood. 'That's my wish,' she said quietly. 'Two wishes, but they're the same wish. What's yours?'

Darcie's face was a mess of tears. 'I want to be the best friend you've ever had,' she said.

Adrien was suddenly very tired and needed her roommate's hand to make it back to the cabin. The short walk seemed interminable. When they finally stumbled through the front door, the rest of the staff were asleep. Taking out a first-aid kit, Darcie cleaned Adrien's hand. 'What's your aunt going to say about this?' she sighed. 'Every time you're around me, you get bashed up. I'm so gutless. I never should've let them put you in that cage. I'm telling you something now, Grouch. I am not going to that camp-fire ever again. I'm staying in bed and getting a good night's sleep. Connor'll be mad, but it's true what you said: shit only works if you believe in it. If you can stand up to him, so can I.' She looked grimly determined, as if her life stood in the balance.

'So you disobey them,' said Adrien, climbing into bed. 'What can they do about it? Their big punishment was to lock me in the Petting Zoo.'

Darcie's eyes turned vague. 'Oh, they do things,' she

said. 'A lot of bullying. Humiliation. Every night, there's some victim. If you don't join in, you become the victim. Everyone's so eager not to be the next victim.'

'I thought it was just good times,' Adrien said faintly.

'It used to be,' said Darcie. 'It wasn't like this last year, when I worked on maintenance. A guy named Ernie led the camp-fires then. He kept it cool, just a place staff could go for a beer. You didn't have to go every night and there wasn't any bullying. I guess it depends on who leads it. Connor was here last year too, doing that grunt thing about your aunt, but it was a just a fun thing then. Not mean like now.'

'It was always mean,' said Adrien. 'He just wasn't in charge.'

'Yeah, I guess,' Darcie said softly. 'I guess we let him take over and change things.' She took a deep breath. 'Well, I'm not going back. We'll stick together, Grouch. What can they do to us if we stick together?'

Adrien turned out the light. 'Maybe they should start worrying about what we could do to them,' she said.

'What could we do?' asked Darcie.

'Ask the Wishing Tree in your dreams,' said Adrien. 'Maybe we'll know by morning.'

Ten

She was floating just under the water's surface, curled into herself. The rhythm of the water was the rhythm of breathing; she rose and fell on the water's breathing as if it was for ever, as if all things could be like this, at peace, waiting for the heart to speak. Slowly, reluctantly, she came awake, her eyes opening. The first thing she noticed was that Darcie's bed was empty – her room-mate was probably getting rid of last night's evidence at the Petting Zoo. Rolling over, Adrien stretched. In spite of missed sleep, she felt soft and warm, full of small yawns. At the back of her mind, she knew she had to decide what to do about Connor, but it was difficult to worry with all this gentleness in her body. The person she really wanted to think about was Paul – she had to talk to him this morning, find out what he had dreamed about last night, if he had lived or died, and how. And she had to make him cough up his birth date, when it was coming, if it was today.

It could be today, she realized. Heartbeat quickening, she showered, then headed to the dining hall. For once she was early. Maybe, she thought, approaching the kitchen door, the hairnets would give her some toast and jam before everyone else came in. If she learned how to say *please* in their weird language, they might even cook her an ecstatic omelette. But just as she placed a hand on the doorknob, about to go in and beg, the sound of whispering caught her ear and she turned to find herself in sudden darkness.

Overhead a crescent moon glimmered, and five familiar girls were gliding past the dining hall into the trees. They were obviously trying to keep quiet – Cath giggled and was immediately shushed – and they seemed intent on something just ahead of them.

'Can you still see her?' Sherry whispered to Roberta, who was leading the way. The five were dressed in nighties and baby dolls. No one had bothered to pull on a sweatshirt.

Roberta nodded. 'This is the same way she came last night,' she hissed. 'I followed her about this far, and then I lost her.'

'She sure ain't going to the bathroom,' observed Nat.

Startled, Adrien realized they were headed towards the camp-fire. It was a different route and there were no white ribbons tied to the trees, but she recognized the area.

'Why would Erin come out here in the middle of the night?' whispered the girl with the long tumble of brown hair.

'Shh,' hissed Sherry and Roberta.

Fire could be seen ahead, flickering through the

143

bush, and the sound of laughter drifted towards the girls. Then the trees opened and a figure stepped from the path into the clearing, pausing so that her wheat-blonde hair caught the firelight in a sudden halo. Friendly cries greeted the young Erin Wood, and a guy moved in and put his arm around her. Someone gave a soft whistle as they kissed.

'Peter Pecker,' whispered Nat with satisfaction.

Intent on watching her aunt, Adrien had forgotten the five girls. Somehow she seemed to have crept in among them, and was surrounded as they crouched together in the dark.

'I told you she was meeting him!' said Nat, triumphant. 'Bet you they don't stay here long.'

Before Nat had even finished her sentence, Erin and the young man had turned and were walking into the trees. 'C'mon,' hissed Roberta, and the girls crept after the pair. The couple didn't go far. The guy spread a blanket and the two lay down together. Hidden among the trees, the girls' breathing took on a quick, short rhythm, their eyes beady and shameless, watching in stunned amazement as clothing came loose, and bodies were naked and joined. The guy kept whispering Erin's name but she seemed to lose all words, the sounds she made, almost singing.

Something rose in Adrien then, too huge to be understood, though she felt it – emotions that swirled like a storm. Lost in it, she turned from what she had seen, what her aunt kept hidden and never let show. Running, she felt as if she was running through trees in the dark, stumbling over roots, branches whipping her face, but when she could think again, she found herself still standing beside the west kitchen entrance as if she had never moved. Above her head the early morning sun slanted down to touch and warm her, and the trees heaved in a slow breeze. She couldn't get the young Erin Wood's joyous cries out of her mind.

She continued to hear them through flag-raising and her aunt's Canada Day speech, and when she joined the staff breakfast line, she was still trying to shake off the wildness that echoed through her. Fortunately, Aunt Erin had disappeared and the assistant director was up front, organizing the entry into the dining hall. Otherwise, Adrien was certain her constant stare would have bored away sections of her aunt's head.

Stepping out of her position further up the line, Darcie walked back to her. 'What's wrong, Grouch?' she asked.

Adrien shrugged. Other staff were watching them closely. Darcie hadn't been seen talking to her since early last week. 'Did you clean up the Petting Zoo?' she said.

Darcie nodded. 'Should we tell your aunt?'

Adrien shot Connor a glance. As usual he was at the front of the line, joking with other staff members. Last night seemed to be forgotten, a trivial event. She thought of what it had meant to her. She had won really, she realized. She had opened cages Connor knew nothing about. 'Y'know,' she said slowly, 'the whole thing was just so stupid.'

'Yeah?' Darcie said dubiously.

'So act like it,' Adrien shrugged. 'If Aunt Erin asks, I was running and I fell on my hand. You bandaged it, right?'

The two girls looked at each other, understanding creeping across Darcie's face. She glanced at Connor. 'He isn't worth it, is he, Grouch?' she said.

'He ain't worth half a sneeze,' said Adrien.

Her roommate nodded again. 'For the first time this summer, I didn't crawl out of bed like a slug,' she sighed. 'And I'm going to sleep all night tonight. Just think of how tomorrow's going to be.'

'Maybe you'll even have time to curl that Spartan hair of yours,' observed Adrien.

Darcie gave a small shriek and covered her hair with her hands. 'I forgot!'

'You missed your face too,' said Adrien.

'My makeup,' whispered Darcie.

Adrien grinned. 'Robin Hood would be proud.'

The maintenance crew held a daily eight-thirty meeting at the east kitchen entrance. Seated on the steps, Adrien was watching for Paul's bike. She was the only member of staff who didn't have to be at her post until nine a.m. Maybe her aunt was going easy on her, she realized. Maybe Aunt Erin did give a thought to stressed-out blood vessels. To her right, most of the maintenance crew had assembled and were listening to Guy's instructions. Paul didn't actually clean toilets – he was usually mowing the lawn or repairing something – but he met with the rest of the crew, and he was usually early. Impatient, Adrien stood and walked over to the group. 'Guy,' she said, trying for casual, 'd'you know where Paul is?'

He gave her a knowing grin. 'Miss him already, eh?'

Adrien took a quick breath, trying to beat the flush rising in her face. 'I just have to talk to him,' she said.

'Probably on his way,' said Guy. 'But get your smooching in quick. We're driving up to Ranch Camp to stock up on supplies.'

Ranch Camp was a programme for advanced horse riders located at a separate campsite, a two-hour drive from Camp Lakeshore. Quickly Adrien headed for the office and caught the screen door just as it was swinging into place behind her aunt. 'When is Paul's birthday?' she demanded, following her in. 'Today?'

Aunt Erin gave her a very blue glance. 'He'll tell you if he wants to.'

'You don't understand,' said Adrien, her voice rising in frustration. 'I have to know.'

'Boy has a right to keep personal information to himself.' Coolly her aunt picked up the phone.

'I hate you!' said Adrien, stamping her foot.

'Mentioned that already,' said Aunt Erin and began dialling. An old phone, it had probably been sitting on the desk since the 1970s – a relic from the past, thought Adrien staring at it, just like her aunt. That cold, distant woman sitting in front of her couldn't possibly connect to the teenager she had heard earlier, giving those uncontrolled cries of wonder in the woods.

'Your clock stopped again,' Adrien said. 'One thirty-seven, just like last time.'

As she turned to look at it, Aunt Erin seemed to stop breathing. 'First cabin comes by Tuck-'n'-Tack at nine thirty,' she said, getting up to fix the clock. 'Best be ready.'

Abruptly Adrien heard the faint whirr of a ten-speed approaching the office. She whirled and ran out, letting the screen door slam behind her. 'Paul!' she yelled from the porch and he braked, then turned and coasted to a stop in front of her. Beneath the tan, his face was pale. Dark smudges shadowed his eyes.

'What's the matter?' she asked. 'Why're you late?'

Slumping forward, he rested his forehead on the handlebars. 'Michelle had to go and visit some puppies down the road,' he said. 'I biked her there first.'

Stupid with relief, she stared at a curl of hair on the nape of his neck. The feeling came to her that she wanted to touch it, curl it around her finger . . . and then she was. Floating strangely through the air, her hand hovered above his neck, then picked up the dark curl and played with it. Sweet heat rushed her face, and she thought she heard soft cries coming from the woods. Quickly she let go of Paul's hair and stood looking at her hand as if it belonged to someone else, someone who could touch those kinds of feelings and hold them close.

He turned his head and rested it on his arms, smiling up at her. She took a deep breath and smiled back. 'What'd you dream about?'

His smile vanished. 'I don't want to talk about it.'

'But you have to tell me,' she said. 'They're my dreams too.'

'No, they're not,' said Paul. Straightening, he started to turn his bike but she stepped in front of him, trapping the wheel between her legs.

'If I'm in them,' she said, 'they're mine.'

Reluctantly, he laughed. 'You're as bad as I am.'

Gripping the handlebars with both hands, she insisted, 'I'm not moving until you tell me.'

His eyes were heavy with fatigue. 'It was both of us this time,' he said.

'How?' she asked.

'It doesn't matter' he said. 'The method's always changing.'

'I want to know,' she said.

Paul's eyes flinched, then held steady. 'We were in a boat with Connor,' he said. 'He tipped it and we were both going down when I woke up.'

'Did Connor?' asked Adrien.

'I didn't notice,' said Paul.

At that moment the office door opened and Aunt Erin stepped out. 'Morning, Paul,' she said.

'Sorry I'm late,' Paul said quickly. 'I had to double-ride Michelle to the neighbor's.'

Aunt Erin simply nodded. Paul gave a gentle tug at his bike but Adrien hung on, resisting her aunt's unspoken order. 'Where's your dirt bike?' she asked.

'I don't take it to work,' he said. 'Could get ripped off.'

Adrien stepped aside and watched as he rode towards the kitchen, ignoring her aunt's pointed silence. Finally she turned to see the screen door being held wide open for her. 'Put out extra T-shirts,' said her aunt. 'Kids always go for T-shirts on their second day at camp.'

Passing under her aunt's arm, Adrien entered the office. 'It's a tradition, right?' she asked.

'Took the words right out of my mouth,' said her aunt, coming in behind her.

All morning long children filed past, pointing to Big Turks or Coffee Crisps, and ordering the occasional T-shirt. Yesterday afternoon, filing cards had been filled out for each camper, listing their spending money, which was stored in the office, and Adrien was kept busy calculating the amount spent, then deducting it from the card. Two or three cabins were scheduled per half-hour, so it was steady but not frenetic. At ten thirty Tamai came through, a row of seven-year-olds following her like ducklings. As the first child peeked over the counter and shyly requested a package of Reese's Pieces, Connor jogged up and barked out an order for Smarties. Wide-eyed, the row of ducklings twisted to look at him.

'Smarties,' Connor repeated, stepping forward.

A memory came to Adrien then, of the little girls touching the Wishing Tree and telling it their secrets. Leaning over the counter, she gently tapped the first girl on the top of her head. 'I think you were interrupted,' she said carefully. 'Here at Tuck-'n'-Tack, everyone waits their turn. Now, what did you wish to order?'

'Reese's Pieces,' the girl whispered.

'Reese's Pieces. My favourite,' said Adrien. 'Here you

are, one package of Reese's Pieces.' She looked at the next girl in line. 'And what would you like?'

Wrinkling her nose, the girl thought fiercely. 'I want an Oh Henry! No, a Smarties, no, a – um, I don't know what I want. I think maybe a Smar – Ni – Mr – Oh, I know, a root beer.'

'Thirsty, eh?' said Adrien. She handed the child a root beer with a smile.

'I'm in a hurry,' snapped Connor.

'I'm not,' said Adrien. With extreme care, she listened to each child's request, then looked at Tamai. 'And what would you like?' she asked. Clustered around their counsellor, the ducklings leaned against her as they carefully unwrapped their treats. Tamai ruffled their hair, one after the other, making sure she touched each one.

'I said I'm in a hurry,' Connor blustered.

'I didn't hear you, Tamai,' said Adrien.

'I've got a class waiting!' said Connor.

'I think,' said Tamai, thinking aloud slowly – *very* slowly, Adrien noted. 'I'll have a Caramilk. No, wait – Nibs.'

'Sure about that?' asked Adrien.

'Yeah, today it'll be the Nibs,' said Tamai. They gave each other wide-open smiles.

'Now where did those Nibs get to?' said Adrien, pottering around the display case.

'Here,' said Connor, stabbing the counter top with his finger.

'What d'you know?' said Adrien. 'Right in their cage where they belong.' She handed the package to Tamai, who gave one last satisfied smile and herded her ducklings away.

'Why is he so mad?' a small voice demanded loudly.

'Oh, he's just grumpy,' said Tamai. 'We're not grumpy, are we?'

'No,' chorused the ducklings.

Adrien couldn't wipe the grin off her face. 'What can I do for you, Grouch?' she asked.

Connor's face burned a slow red. 'Smarties, smart ass,' he hissed.

'Here you are,' she said brightly, handing him a package. 'Have a nice day.'

Stepping closer, he spoke quickly. 'I saw Darcie let you out,' he said in a low voice. 'You think I really would've left you there all night? I was just about to let you out myself when she showed up.'

Adrien watched narrow-eyed as he fidgeted nervously with the Smarties package. 'You didn't have the key,' she said. 'Darcie had it.'

His eyes flickered. 'I would've gone and got her,' he said. 'That's just what I was going to do when she showed up and got you out.'

Abruptly a cabin of boys rounded the corner. Eight-year-olds crowded in around Connor and plastered their faces to the display case. On their heels, their counsellor paused, glancing from Connor to Adrien.

'Who's first?' Adrien asked, and the boys let loose with a chorus of 'Me, me, me!' Without another word, Connor turned and jogged off. As she watched him go, Adrien felt as if she had been unplugged from an electrical circuit. The relief that flooded her was so great, she almost dropped to the floor.

'You all right?' asked the counsellor, pushing through the boys and leaning over the counter. 'You're awfully pale.'

Laying her face on the counter, Adrien let the dizziness pass. 'Yeah, sure. I'm okay.'

The counsellor ordered his shoving, yapping group into a line and turned back to her. 'I heard about what happened last night,' he said. 'I wasn't there because I'm a counsellor, but I can tell you — most of us don't like it.'

'You don't?' said Adrien, staring.

'No.' The counsellor looked around uneasily, as if expecting Connor or Bunter to leap out at him from behind a tree. He wore glasses and looked like the studious type. 'Staff are talking,' he informed her. 'They're pissed off. The whole thing's getting out of hand.'

The boy waiting at the head of the line gave the counsellor a shove. The counsellor shoved him back. 'Wait your turn,' he ordered. 'I'm first. I'll take an Oh Henry! and a Coke.'

'Stop going to the camp-fire,' Adrien said as she handed him the candy. 'Let Connor sit there by himself.'

'I don't have to go while I've got this rat pack,' said the counsellor, 'but I rotate to maintenance next week.' Turning, he glared at the squirming line of boys. 'Would you rodents keep quiet for one second?' The boys made terrified faces and froze, staring at him. Giving a heavy sigh, the counsellor turned back to Adrien.

'I'll think about it,' he said. 'Everyone's thinking about it, actually.'

The day seemed suddenly to change colours. It had never occurred to Adrien that everyone might secretly be on her side. Slightly stunned, she gave the boys their candy, then watched the weary counsellor lead his yapping pack towards the mini-golf course. Somehow she had forgotten the most important thing: staff weren't robots. Each one had a free-thinking mind, and it looked as if some of them might actually start using it.

On her fifteen-minute break, she used the office phone to call home and wish her parents a happy Canada Day. Her mother answered. For some inexplicable reason, Adrien felt as if they hadn't spoken in years. They talked in rushes, their voices weaving in and out of each other. 'I'm okay,' Adrien kept saying. 'Everything's fine, I'm not over-exerting myself. Aunt Erin has me on the easiest schedule of anyone.'

She didn't know how to get past her mother's questions to tell her: *Something's changing, Mom. Something deep and sleepy inside me is starting to wake up.* So she simply said, 'I fell and cut my hand, but my roommate Darcie fixed it. My roommate's the archery instructor. She hits a bull's-eye every single time.'

She said goodbye three times before her mother let her go. Then she stood, one hand resting on the phone, letting the latest truth settle in. The phone call had been good. For the first time in two years, she had *wanted* to talk to her mother. Their voices had merged and run together – she couldn't remember half the things they had said. What stayed with her was the feel of her mother's voice, the tone of it – the love her mother felt for her, the love she felt back. At home in Saskatoon, she knew her mother was probably crying with relief. When she finished, Adrien thought hopefully, she might relax and breathe a little deeper, smile a few times. Perhaps she would even be able to let the day be more than constant worry, the sickening lurch of fear.

Glancing up from the computer, Aunt Erin asked, 'How's your mom?'

Adrien had forgotten her aunt was in the office. Turning to stare out of the window, she felt hundreds of tiny inner hooks let go and slip free. How she had *worried* about her mother, she realized.

'She's good,' she said slowly. 'I think she'll be all right.'

Aunt Erin's smile changed her whole face. 'Glad to hear it,' she said heartily. 'Think I'll ever get my sweat-shirt back?'

'Maybe if the Tories get re-elected,' said Adrien.

Aunt Erin grimaced. 'She can keep it. Now head on out there, you've got kids waiting.'

'Yes, boss,' Adrien said, and stepped out to serve the children.

Eleven

As Adrien was closing Tuck-'n'-Tack for lunch, Darcie came by with a large paper bag. 'Din-din,' she said, shaking it. 'I told the cooks you were helping me fix arrows.'

'And they bought it?' demanded Adrien.

'Well, you are,' said Darcie. With a menacing look, she picked up the whistle she wore around her neck.

Adrien covered her ears and cowered. 'Not the whistle, not the whistle,' she moaned.

As they walked to the archery range, they passed a group of children coming back from the corrals, but otherwise it was a quiet walk through rustling trees. The range was empty, just the equipment shed at one end and the targets at the other. Picking up the bag, Adrien snooped through it while Darcie unlocked the shed and brought out a canister of damaged arrows.

'Beans,' Adrien announced, opening two warm Tupperware containers. 'It's Canada Day and they give us sausages and beans.'

'Glad I'm working out here all afternoon,' said Darcie, sitting down beside her. 'Can you imagine being cooped up with a pack of little farts in Arts and Crafts?'

'Farts and Crafts,' said Adrien, remembering. Companionably they dug into their beans. 'This must be the cheapest way to feed a couple of hundred kids.'

'Yeah, but it's healthy,' said Darcie. 'Maybe it'll improve their brain activity. One idiot was tearing the feathers off an arrow this morning. Complete barbarian.'

'Did you blow your whistle?' asked Adrien.

'I blew his head off,' said Darcie. 'You'd think kids would have some appreciation for the finesse of this sport. It's supposed to be quiet and peaceful. Zennish, like meditation. The power of the mind –'

'– over a circle pinned to a straw bale,' finished Adrien, then noticed a distinctly huffy quality developing about Darcie's mouth. 'You've got very nice trees around here,' she added hastily. 'Lovely atmosphere for mind-over-matter stuff.'

Darcie gave her a suspicious glance, then decided to give her the benefit of the doubt. 'You should see the professional ranges,' she said.

'That what you're going to be when you grow up?' asked Adrien. 'A professional Robin Hood?'

'I'm not good enough,' said Darcie. 'I can hit a straw bale, but . . . What're you going to do?'

'You mean if I don't keel over first?' said Adrien. Somehow she had never given much thought to a professional career. 'Maybe I'll work in a funeral home. Become a mortician. Find out how everything looks inside, how each organ works to keep you alive.'

Darcie paused, then said carefully, 'I don't know if that'd really suit you, Grouch. They don't allow a sense of humour in funeral homes. You'd have to ditch all your snappy comebacks. Why not work in a nursery, with itty-bitty newborn babies? That'd teach you a lot more about how the body's alive, wouldn't it?'

Adrien sat watching the trees play with shadow and light. She had never held a baby, she thought wonderingly. What would it be like to hold a tiny life that didn't even know it was possible to die? 'You think different from me,' she said grudgingly.

Darcie scraped up the last of her beans. 'Yeah,' she agreed, 'but I'm a limited thinker compared to you. I can tell. You've got the kind of mind that travels to other planets, like the Doomsday Man.'

'Paul Marchand?' Adrien said quickly.

'You're blushing,' Darcie said softly. 'It's okay, I already know you're crazy about him.'

Adrien wanted to scramble to her feet and leave. Why did everyone have to tease? she thought fervently. Was it the summer camp mentality? 'Promise you won't ever bug me about this,' she said, staring fiercely at a bull's-eye.

'Yeah, sure,' Darcie said easily. 'Cross my heart, hope to –'

'Die,' Adrien said, looking directly at her. Darcie's eyes faltered, and then she nodded. 'Have you ever had a boyfriend?' Adrien asked.

Darcie switched to the non-death topic with relief. 'Yeah, a couple. Not all at once, of course.'

'So, uh, how far did you go?' asked Adrien.

Darcie looked startled. 'You mean sex?'

Adrien nodded.

'I've never had *sex*,' admitted Darcie. 'Yet. Came pretty close a few times, but that's as far as I wanted to go. It has to be right, y'know. You have to feel right about it. It's important, letting someone touch you.' She paused. 'You and Paul haven't –'

'No.' Adrien shook her head. 'It's just . . . it feels so strong. Like if we just kissed, we'd go all the way, y'know?'

Darcie smiled knowingly. 'Yeah, but it's not like that,' she assured. 'Feelings are strong, but you've still got a mind. You can take it in stages. Have fun with it. Play.'

'Have fun?' said Adrien, stunned. *Play?* The whole thing seemed so serious, almost like a pact with death.

'Look, Grouch,' said Darcie. 'You're going to have a ton of boyfriends. I can tell. You'll have a lot more than me. Paul's a nice guy, but you're not marrying him – just making out.'

Adrien heaved an enormous sigh. How could she possibly explain to Darcie what was going on between Paul and herself? 'I just really like him,' she said.

'You go all gooey every time you see him,' smiled Darcie.

'I do?' Adrien was horrified.

'So does he,' Darcie soothed. 'He sees you and he loses his knees. Don't worry, it happens to everyone. Now, see this arrow here? This is how you glue a feather onto a shaft. Are you watching carefully, Grouch?'

'Yeah, I'm watching,' said Adrien. 'But I'm not fixing any of your precious arrows, Spart. I can't concentrate. I'm getting hot flashes.'

'That bad, eh?' said Darcie.

'Yeah,' sighed Adrien.

'So next time you see him,' Darcie advised breezily, 'jump on him.'

All afternoon she handed out this or that chocolate bar. All afternoon she sat with her head cocked, listening for the sound of Guy's pickup coming down the road. Time stretched, endless as the horizon across the lake. By the time the pickup finally pulled into the parking lot, everyone had gone into the dining hall for supper. Getting up from the office steps where she had been waiting, Adrien watched Paul climb out of the truck.

'C'mon in and get some supper before you head home,' said Guy. 'Hey – Paul!'

Instead of responding, Paul stood, one hand on the pickup's wing and stared at Adrien. All she seemed to be able to do was stare back. Removing his black cowboy hat, Guy shook his head. 'He's all yours,' he said, coming towards Adrien. 'Been thinking about you all day. Must be true love – I couldn't get a word out of him.'

He walked away, leaving the two of them watching each other over the pickup. 'Can we go for a smoke?' Adrien asked. 'Or d'you want to get some supper?'

Paul shook his head, then said quietly, 'I should get my bike.'

They walked silently into the woods, the whirr of

the bike between them. Adrien felt hollow and hungry, and wondered what the hairnets were serving for supper. Leaning his bike against a tree, Paul dug for his cigarettes in the pocket of his lumber jacket. Silently she shook her head at him and his hand froze. She stepped towards him. Close. Closer. Now she could see the pores in his skin, the tiny creases in his lips. Sudden warmth flowed through her and she wanted to touch him, she wanted –

'Whoa!' said Paul, stepping back. 'C'mon, Adrien, I told you – my head's too crazy right now. Don't bug me.' Grabbing his bike, he swung it onto the path. Then he mounted and pedalled off, leaving her standing alone in the shock of her skin.

She wandered the woods for hours, drifting with the dying light, touching the bark of trees. *Adrien – don't bug me*, she heard over and over in her head. *Don't bug me*. Just this morning, she had touched his hair and he had smiled up at her. She could remember the exact curve of his lips, the lines at the corner of his mouth. Where had that smile gone now? she wondered despairingly. How had she made him change, what had she done wrong? Sick with a deep ache, she couldn't imagine seeing him again, walking towards him, talking to him. Stupid, she had been so *stupid*, and Darcie and Guy had been wrong. Paul didn't love her, no one loved her, and she would die before anyone ever did because there was no way she was ever believing in love again – it hurt way too much.

As evening darkened, she came out onto the shore

and walked along the lonely dock. Further down the beach, the older children were at a singalong camp-fire. The younger ones were already in bed. Hours back she had lost her hunger and now she sat dull-eyed and vacant, staring across the grey-blue water to where the spirits drifted, their bodies glowing as they slept. What good were they? she wondered as she watched them. They never did anything, never sent her any messages, never spoke. What did they matter, what did anything matter? A hot tear slid down her cheek.

Behind her, laughter came dancing out of the night trees. Glancing over her shoulder, Adrien saw five girls coming down the path to the beach, their pale bodies wrapped in towels. Amid whispers and giggles, they stepped onto the dock.

Adrien felt a clutch at her throat. There wasn't enough room, she thought, panicking. What should she do – jump off the dock and watch from the water? Trapped in indecision, she scooted to one side and watched as the girls paused a foot from her, looking at one another.

'Now!' said Roberta, and all five dropped their towels. The moon lit every curve of their naked bodies as they stood shifting hesitantly on the dock.

'This is embarrassing,' said Cath.

'No, it isn't.' Roberta stretched out her arms. 'It's glorious. The air's kissing my skin everywhere.'

'I'm going in,' said Nat. Taking several running steps, she dived into the water, followed by Sherry's cannon-ball. Cath slipped in slowly as Roberta dropped off the edge, standing to attention. The last girl spun and dropped in backwards, her face frightened. As Adrien stared, the water closed over her head like dread and she came up fighting.

'Over here, Debbie,' Roberta called. The girl swam out to her and was promptly ducked. 'This feels so cool,' sang Roberta. 'I hate swimsuits. I'm never wearing one again.'

The girls splashed and dog-paddled, floated on their backs, and counted stars. Even Debbie seemed to relax, losing her look of fear.

Adrien couldn't stop watching their bodies. Their breasts floated gently in the water, their buttocks flashed in the darkness, going under, surfacing again. It was like a dance, she thought, the girls playing with the water, letting it touch and stroke them – some kind of utter freedom she had never imagined.

'What d'you think Erin is doing now?' Roberta called as she came paddling towards the dock.

'D'you mean what is she doing, or *exactly* what is she doing?' Nat called back.

Roberta giggled. 'It's a good thing she doesn't know we sneak out while she's gone. Otherwise she'd have to be responsible and lonely all night in her bed.'

'Thinking about Peter Pecker,' sang Sherry.

Without warning Roberta surfaced directly in front of Adrien, grasped the dock firmly, and hauled herself out of the water. Twisting, she planted her butt exactly where Adrien was sitting, then leaned back, shaking the water out of her hair. Rigid and disbelieving, Adrien sat holding her breath as the other girl continued to lean back on her hands, legs splayed, splashing one foot in the water. Gradually Adrien let herself relax. As she did, she began to feel the other girl's body all around her own. With a start she realized Roberta was humming. Tiny vibrations rippled through her chest, there was the steady thud of her heart, the quiet lift and fall of her rib cage as she breathed, the cool slide of water over her foot. Adrien could even feel the air shifting along the girl's wet skin. She had never known skin could feel so alive, she thought wonderingly. It was like an entire forest rippling in a slow breeze. If only she could read Roberta's mind . . . Letting her head fall back like the other girl's, Adrien saw the vast panorama of the night sky, its wild sprinkling of stars and the shadowy green glimmer of the Northern Lights.

'We should stop wearing bras,' Roberta declared, suddenly leaning forward. 'Ditch *all* our underwear.'

'Like women's libbers?' called Sherry.

'We'll string them up the flagpole,' declared Nat, swimming small circles.

'Bras are different,' Cath said. 'Everyone can tell you're not wearing one. You jiggle.'

'You're supposed to jiggle,' said Roberta, jerking her shoulders so her breasts swung. 'We'll have a Jiggle Revolution.'

Giggling, Sherry cupped her own breasts and jiggled them. Soon the other girls were following suit. Then Nat dived underwater and the Jiggle Revolution ended.

'I hate the way my boobs move when I walk,' said

Debbie, up to her neck in water. 'I always try to keep them, y'know, solid, like a guy's chest, so I don't get embarrassed.'

'Plastic Barbie tits,' agreed Sherry.

'It's embarrassing, the way guys stare,' said Cath.

'They're just jealous,' said Roberta. 'I'm going to stick my tits out like a wooden mermaid on a ship's prow.' Lifting herself up on her hands, she dropped back into the water.

Immediately the scene began to fade. *No*, Adrien thought. *Please don't go.* Desperately she hung on to what she could see: pale white flashes that glowed eerily in the water. Then she realized she was seeing two sets of girls, their bodies and their spirits, swimming together like dolphins, diving and surfacing, weaving around each other in a kind of caress, though they never quite touched – the girls seemed unaware of the spirits, feeling their presence only as a loose, shifting joy.

Gradually the scene faded completely, leaving Adrien staring at the empty water. Above her, the sky was still light and a few stars had come out. Down the beach, the camp-fire was breaking up. Abruptly she felt solidly, ravenously hungry, and stood slowly, feeling every fibre in her body, a forest rippling quietly in her skin. As she climbed the path and crossed the lawn, she wondered who would take pity and feed her this late. Then she saw her aunt come out of the office and lean on the railing.

'Paul called for you,' she said. 'Several times. Wants you to call him back. You can use the office phone.'

'Could I borrow a quarter?' asked Adrien. She simply *couldn't* have this conversation in front of anyone, especially her aunt. Digging a quarter out of her jeans, Aunt Erin dropped it over the rail. Then she gave Adrien the phone number and went back into the office. Slowly Adrien headed for the camp's payphone and punched in the number.

'Hello?' Paul's voice sounded husky, raw.

'Hi,' Adrien whispered.

'Adrien?' he asked.

'Yeah,' she whispered.

He paused and she waited, teetering on the edge of everything.

'It's not that I don't like you,' he said finally. 'I like you a lot more than Leanne. It's just that everything's like fire, burning so vivid. Everything I want is on the other side of my birthday. I've got to wait until then, okay?'

'I don't know when your birthday is,' she said. 'My brain could blow. I could be dead by then.'

'No,' he said quickly. 'You're always there. I dream it.'

She thought of the five girls, the joy in their bodies, the laughter they carried everywhere. The way they had dropped their towels. 'I'm going to kiss you tomorrow,' she said, and listened to his breathing quicken.

'Adrien —' he faltered.

'Paul, did you make Leanne do it?' she asked.

'No!' he exploded.

'Then maybe *she* was the one who made the mistake,' said Adrien. 'Maybe she didn't know enough to say no.'

'Maybe,' said Paul. 'I think I knew that, though. I just had my head in some fucked-up place.'

'Okay, so you both fucked up,' she said. 'It didn't kill you. Or her.'

'Yeah, okay,' he said quietly.

'And –' She thought of the girls again and swallowed. 'Well,' she said slowly, 'I'm here *now*.'

'Yeah.' He was smiling, she could hear it. 'You sure are.'

'Will you kiss me back?' she asked hoarsely. 'I've never kissed anyone. I don't know how to do it.'

He gave a quiet laugh, then said, 'You catch on quick. Don't worry.'

A soft, easy breath lifted through her. 'I won't then,' she said. 'Worry.'

'This is going to be one long sweaty night,' he muttered. 'See you tomorrow.'

'Yeah,' she whispered. 'See you tomorrow.'

Hanging up the phone, she stood in the booth's white light, listening to her heart beat – a promise repeating itself, becoming truer each time it spoke.

Twelve

The master cabin was a one-bedroom apartment, equipped with a kitchenette and a bathroom. The main room held a sofa, stereo and bookshelf at one end, the tiny kitchen, a card table and several stacking chairs at the other. No TV could be seen anywhere. Telling Adrien to sit down, Aunt Erin got some cold meatloaf, mustard, and milk out of the fridge and fixed her a sandwich.

'Drink the milk,' she said. 'Good for you.'

As Adrien ate, her aunt sat across the table, toying with a piece of bread. Adrien waited for a barrage of questions about missing supper and wandering the woods all evening, but there was no interrogation, no advice. Maybe her aunt felt she had none to give.

'Paul and I,' Adrien said into the silence, 'had a sort of not-fight fight, but I guess we're okay now.'

'Weren't at flag-lowering tonight.' Dull-eyed, Aunt Erin watched her own fingers tear at the bread. Her shoulders were slumped and her breathing seemed laboured. Adrien hesitated, then decided to open a door.

'Aunt Erin,' she asked, 'have you ever been in love?'

Her aunt's eyes widened. Dropping her face into her hands, she rubbed it. 'Yes,' she said quietly.

Adrien watched her carefully. 'It's confusing, isn't it?'

'Yes,' her aunt said again, not looking up.

'But I think I like it,' Adrien admitted.

'Paul's a boy of honour,' said her aunt. 'Couldn't find a better young man. Just remember your whole life's ahead of you.'

Like you did? Adrien thought, then asked, 'Could I use your toilet?'

The bathroom was tiny, just a shower stall, toilet and sink. The walls seemed thin, and she wondered how cold the room got in winter. Aunt Erin was a true Spartan. As the toilet flushed, Adrien carefully opened the medicine cabinet. While she had been sick, she had seen a biographer explain to a TV talk show host that whenever he interviewed Hollywood stars in their homes, he always checked their medicine cabinets because that was where people kept their secrets. Immediately Adrien found what she was looking for: two prescription bottles, one for sleeping pills and the other for Prozac. So, she thought, staring at the second label, Aunt Erin was on anti depressants. And if she was mixing them with sleeping medication, it was no wonder she hadn't heard her niece yelling from the Petting Zoo.

Closing the medicine cabinet, Adrien scanned the bathroom for more details and spotted a bottle of blonde hair dye in the shower stall. So, she thought again, her aunt was keeping the grey out of her hair, pretending to stay young. Living in the past. Emerging from the bathroom, she found Aunt Erin still at the table, picking at the piece of bread.

'Aunt Erin,' Adrien said. 'Those girls in the photograph – who were they?'

'Just a cabin of girls I counselled,' said her aunt.

'But why d'you keep their picture where you can always see it?' asked Adrien.

'Something I need to do.'

Adrien didn't know what to tell the depressed woman sitting in front of her – that the girls had been more alive than anyone she had ever known? That they had been happy, their bodies had hummed with a music most people never heard? Her aunt already knew that.

'I'm glad you asked me here this summer,' she said slowly. 'I'm learning.'

Her aunt looked up, a quick gladness in her face. 'Good. Now, time for bed. Your mother'd be having a fit.'

The knock came at around one a.m., waking them both. 'Whaaaaaaat?' Darcie moaned into her pillow. 'I thought I was going to get some sleeeeeeep.'

The door opened and the hall light shone into the cabin bedroom. Rolling over, Adrien squinted at the dark shape leaning in the brightly lit doorway. 'Darcie,' said a female voice, 'you coming?'

'No,' mumbled Darcie.

'Why not?' said the voice.

'I want to sleeeeeeep,' said Darcie.

There was a pause. 'The rest of us want to sleeeeeeep too,' said the voice.

'Then go to bed,' said Darcie.

'They'll get us,' said a second dark shape pushing in beside the first one, 'if we're alone in our own rooms.'

The doorway was now crowded with girls. With a sigh, Darcie sat up. 'Geeeeeeez,' she groaned. 'Bring your mattresses in and put them on the floor.'

'We'll have to sleep double,' said someone.

'C'mon, Grouch,' said Darcie. 'If I have to sleep with someone, it's going to be you.'

Quickly Adrien scooted across the small room and climbed into Darcie's bed. As the other girls brought in two mattresses, she plumped her pillow, then snuggled and burrowed until she was comfortably warm and happy, surrounded by the scent of Darcie's perfume.

'Hey,' complained her roommate. 'I didn't say I wanted to play teddy bears. And do you mind? I'm plastered against the wall.'

'I like your bed.' Adrien had the giggles.

'Well, you can like my bed facing the other way,' said Darcie. 'Then there'll be some room for me.'

Obligingly Adrien turned to face the room, and Darcie got comfortable behind her. The other girls seemed to be doing the same, shifting and sighing on their mattresses. 'What d'you think they'll do to us?' asked someone nervously.

'What can they do to eight girls in one room?' Darcie said scornfully.

'Well, you know all those school shootings —' said a voice.

'Connor doesn't have a gun,' Darcie said emphatically. 'Besides, he's not the loner type. Mass murderers are loners. Ever see him alone? He's a wild partier.'

'Anyway,' added Adrien, 'we've got Robin Hood.'

'Hey, Darcie!' said someone. 'Tomorrow, bring your bow and arrow to bed.'

'You're not sleeping in here tomorrow!' exclaimed Darcie.

'Oh yes we are,' chorused the other girls.

Darcie muttered into her pillow. Gradually the breathing in the room evened out until it seemed an extension of the night sighing through the trees.

'Spart, you awake?' asked Adrien.

In reply, Darcie's arm lifted and came around Adrien, patting her shoulder. 'See what you started?' she said. 'Freedom. A revolution.'

'One of the guy counsellors talked to me this morning,' said Adrien. 'He said a lot of staff are mad about the cage thing.'

'I think Connor's going to fizzle like a popped balloon,' said Darcie.

'Weird, eh? Sure didn't feel like it a couple of days ago,' said Adrien.

Darcie patted her shoulder again. 'People just need an example, Grouch. You're a hero.'

Adrien squirmed slightly. She was getting happier and happier. 'I like all of us sleeping in one room.'

'I sure hope no one snores,' muttered Darcie.

'Y'know, Spart, I could die in this bed before morning,' Adrien teased sleepily.

'You're giving me the willies,' said Darcie.

'If I did, I'd shit my pants,' Adrien added.

'Honest, Grouch,' complained Darcie, 'how'm I supposed to sleep, thinking –'

Adrien fell asleep.

At flag-raising Connor stood poker-stiff, staring straight ahead. When Bunter spoke to him in the breakfast line, he gave terse replies, then fell back into his thoughts. Whispers travelled up and down the staff line as stories were traded about last night. It sounded as if more than half the staff had opted for sleep, and the camp-fire had been a desultory affair. Initially cautious, staff members standing close to Connor began to relax. When jokes were told, the laughter came out differently, less like a chorus. By lunch everyone had stopped shooting glances in his direction, as if asking for permission to act like individuals. Darcie's prediction was coming true, Adrien realized. Connor was fizzling like a popped balloon.

She, on the other hand, felt like an over-pumped balloon. At eight thirty she had seen Paul, and they had agreed to meet again at four. All day she thought about the expression on his face. Was she being stupid, or had he smiled enough? she wondered. Had he really touched her hand, or had she just imagined it? Last night on the phone his voice had been so raw, and this morning when he first saw her, he had taken one quick breath as if he had suddenly run short of air.

Finally the last cabin came through Tuck-'n'-Tack and she was free. Paul showed up and helped her close, then waited while she took in the till. As they walked into the woods, he took her good hand. Heat pulsed between their palms. One of the last mayflies fluttered into his hair and rested, catching the light in its wings, but she left it there.

'What did you dream about last night?' she asked.

'You,' he said, squeezing her hand.

'Did I die?'

'No,' was all he said, and a warm flush crept up both their faces. Stopping in the clearing he had taken her to for their first smoke, Paul started to pull out his pack of cigarettes, but Adrien shook her head.

'You quit?' he asked.

'I don't feel like it right now,' she said.

Shoving the pack nervously into his pocket, Paul removed his lumber jacket and dropped it under a tree. 'Okay, um, let's see,' he said, looking around. 'Usually, before you get to the, uh, kissing part, you do something else – bowling, biking, dancing. I thought maybe we could dance.'

'Dance?' squeaked Adrien. She hadn't been to a school dance since grade eight. She couldn't remember a *thing* about dancing.

'It's easy,' said Paul. Now that she looked petrified, he appeared a little less so. 'C'mere,' he grinned. When she didn't move, he stepped close, slid one arm around her waist, and took her hand. Hesitantly she put her other hand on his shoulder. All over, her skin was coming alive with feelings. Paul spoke into her ear.

'I'll be the music. All we have to do is shuffle.' He started to hum low in his throat. 'Got any favourites?'

Adrien was getting the giggles again. 'The bullfrog one,' she said. 'Jeremiah with the wine.'

'That's an oldie,' said Paul. 'I don't know all the words, but I know the tune.' He hummed along, his voice wavering huskily, and it helped that he couldn't sing well. With Paul, thought Adrien, things were raw-edged and honest – nothing had to be perfect. As they shuffled around the clearing, they were so close she could feel the vibrations of his voice in his throat and chest, and his breath ruffled her hair. Gradually her tension slid away, she closed her eyes and let her body follow his. When he finished singing about Jeremiah, he started another oldie, one she recognized but couldn't name. Opening her eyes, she watched his mouth. It was so close, she thought. When was it going to happen? When were they finally going to kiss?

Paul opened his eyes. 'Okay, enough dancing,' he said, then looked around again. 'I want this to be the best first kiss in the history of mankind.'

'Paul, the suspense is killing me,' said Adrien.

'You'll live.' He pulled her to a tree and they sat down with their backs to it. Carefully he took her damaged hand and traced Darcie's bandage. 'So, uh, what d'you think camels look like when they're kissing?' he asked casually.

She saw it, and a shout of laughter burst out of her.

'Snakes?' he added.

Giggles bounced around Adrien's insides. 'Walruses,' she snorted.

Paul grinned. 'Anteaters with their snaky little tongues.' He plucked a stem of seed grass. 'Hold still.'

The laughter had changed her whole body. Adrien felt like water, fluid and sparkling, and smiled as Paul touched the grass tip to her lower lip. As he drifted it across, a sweet tickle sent itself everywhere through her. He did it again.

'Oh,' she whispered. 'That's incredible.'

Smiling, he traced the grass across her cheek, her throat. Then he leaned closer and kissed her chin. 'Hey,' he said, 'I thought you were going to kiss me.'

She had never imagined it could be like this – talking, laughing, playing – as if the entire purpose was just to make each other happy. Taking the seed grass, she traced it gently across his mouth. Eyes closed, Paul sat leaning against the tree, his body giving the tiniest shudder each time she tickled his lips with the grass. Her skin seemed to be humming, as if her body had become a kind of music, and she felt as if she could spend the rest of her life touching his mouth. His lips were the colour of a ripe peach. Dropping the grass, she brushed her lips across his once, like a whisper. Paul moaned, and without thinking, without telling herself to, she simply touched her mouth full to his. His lips were soft and moved in small ripples so they were kissing endless tiny kisses, her body full of soft bursting questions. *How will this feel? How will this make him feel?*

Each question asked the next. She wanted to know so much. She felt as if she was discovering the reason her body lived.

Finally Paul pulled her face into his neck and they sat together, hearts pounding, letting their breathing slow.

'Thank you,' she whispered.

'For what?' he murmured.

'For thinking about it first,' she said.

'I've been thinking about it from the first minute I saw you,' he said, tugging gently on her hair. 'But, uh, Adrien, I'm real close to splitting my jeans, okay?'

Realizing what he meant, she sat up. Inches from hers, Paul's face was flushed, his eyes almost closed. As she saw it, a heavy heat blew through her, heat that was almost pain, heat she wasn't yet ready for. Reluctantly she got to her feet. About her, the clearing was dusty with late-afternoon light. Stretching her arms, she drifted in a slow circle.

'Adrien,' said Paul.

She stopped and looked at him. The world was still spinning slightly, Paul standing at its centre and staring past her. Following his gaze, she turned to see what he was looking at. Initially, all she noticed was the green-gold air, full of slight vibrations. Then she caught sight of an opening, she was sure she could *feel* an opening to some other place pulsing mid-air in front of her. Slowly she stretched out a hand to touch it. The pulsing felt like music. She wanted to hear it.

'No!' cried Paul, pulling her back. Wrapped in his arms, Adrien felt dazed, distant, her head full of strange light. The violence of his heartbeats thudded through them both.

'Never do that,' he whispered. 'They were reaching for you.'

His fear ran around them in circles. Sleepily she yawned and waited for it to subside.

'Promise you won't do that again,' he said, letting her go. 'Never reach for them. If they want you, they'll take hold and pull you through.'

'All right,' she said, but she couldn't understand his fear. The vision before her had felt so beautiful, like a dream from which she was just waking. Softly she touched Paul's mouth and he sighed.

'Just think,' he said. 'Life could go on like this, day after day after day.'

Thirteen

Adrien was restless. It was evening, everyone on the staff was involved with programmed activities except her, and all she could think about was Paul. Leaving the cabin, she drifted towards the lake. On her arrival at the beach, she saw that the spirits were their usual soft glow, floating on the water's surface. *Wait a minute*, Adrien thought, her pulse quickening. *They're floating just under the surface, not on it. The way I do in my dreams.* As she stared, the lapping waves blurred the spirits' glowing outlines, and she realized she had seen them awake several times only – twice when the weather had been stormy, and yesterday when they had joined the girls to skinny-dip in the lake. They seemed to spend most of their time sleeping. What did they dream about? Adrien wondered as she watched them. The brief week they had been alive at Camp Lakeshore? Was that why she kept seeing the five girls – the sleeping spirits were sending her their memories? But why her? No one else seemed to experience their dreams, not even Paul. Did Aunt Erin?

With a sigh, she wandered over to Prairie Sky and leaned against an outer wall, swatting mosquitoes. A group of eight-year-olds passed by on a nature walk, and shrieks from a game of Capture the Flag echoed through the woods. Abruptly she heard Nat's voice, coming from inside the cabin.

'If you tell, we'll kill you.'

Moving to a window, she peered through it. Inside, the light was on and she could see eight girls facing off in two groups – five on one side, three on the other.

'You don't scare me, Nat,' said one of the three. 'I'm still telling.'

'But you'll get Erin into trouble,' Debbie said pleadingly.

'She should get into trouble.' The girl crossed her arms defensively. 'She's supposed to be here at night, looking after us. And you're not supposed to be out there, running around.'

'Why not?' demanded Sherry, stepping forward, her hands on her hips, and the three girls shuffled backwards bumping into each other.

'Because it's not safe,' blustered one of the three.

'What's not safe?' scoffed Nat. 'The moon? The trees?'

'What if a man saw you?' asked a girl.

'Here at camp?' demanded Nat. 'Anyway, what's one guy going to do to all of us?'

Closest to the window, Roberta stood pulling nervously at her hair. Cath and Debbie sat on a nearby bunk, their gaze darting from Nat to the three girls.

Debbie chewed her nails. Sherry and Nat leaned forward in full battle position, glaring.

'I'll find out where you live,' Nat threatened. 'I'll track you down. I'll –'

'Why don't you come with us?' Roberta interrupted. 'We never said you couldn't come.'

'I don't want to go out in the dark,' said one of the three. 'And you're not allowed. You're breaking the rules. Erin's letting you and she's a bad counsellor.'

'She is not.' Enraged, Sherry shoved her face into the other girl's. 'She's in love.'

'Well, she's not supposed to be,' the girl said flatly.

'She doesn't know we go out,' protested Cath. 'It's not her fault. We sneak out after she leaves.'

'You wouldn't even know she goes out,' said Roberta, 'except we woke you last night by accident.'

'I bet you sneak out to meet the boys,' said the girl farthest from Sherry, her eyes narrowed, her arms also crossed.

'No,' Debbie said quickly. 'We do stuff on our own.'

'You were skinny-dipping,' the same girl accused.

A tiny smile crossed Nat's face. 'How long did you watch?' she asked, her tone coy, knowing.

The other girl froze, and Nat closed in.

'Did you like watching us skinny-dip, Lesley?' she added sweetly.

'I just heard you and wanted to see what you were doing,' muttered Lesley. She was losing ground rapidly and everyone knew it. Her eyes faltered and she began to turn away.

'I think you liked it,' Nat hissed, stepping forward. 'Lesley the Lez. If you tell anyone about Erin or us being out at night, I'll tell everyone you spied on us because you like girls.'

'We didn't spy on you,' said one of the others, trying to bolster Lesley. 'You could've been in trouble or something.'

'No one'll believe that after the story we tell about you three,' said Nat, her voice now calm, tasting victory.

'I'm with Nat,' smiled Sherry, twisting her ponytail. 'We'll tell everyone, right, Debbie?'

'Right,' said Debbie.

'Right, Cath?' asked Sherry.

'Right,' agreed Cath.

'What about you, Robi?' asked Sherry.

Roberta finally nodded, and the air changed. For a moment the three girls stared at her, then slowly moved apart. From this point on, anything they did together would be suspect: talking, laughing, even looking at each other. Nat had come up with the perfect accusation.

'Only a lez would want to stop Erin from seeing her boyfriend,' Nat said with a satisfied smile, and the scene vanished, leaving Adrien on tiptoe, stiff from straining to see in. She was about to let go of the window ledge when suddenly another scene took shape before her. This time the three girls were lying silently in their bunks and Roberta was standing in the centre of the dark cabin, holding a flashlight.

'I don't think you're lezzes,' she was saying. 'Anyway, who cares if you are? It's all just love, isn't it?'

'It's dirty and it's a lie,' said one of the girls.

Roberta hesitated, then blurted, 'I'm sorry Nat made you feel bad. She was really scared that you'd tell on Erin. Erin's . . . the best counsellor I ever had. She's just the best. And she's in love. Haven't you ever been in love? Mad-crazy for someone? I can tell you how it feels – like the grass, sky and air are whispering and touching each other. You're so happy, you can hardly breathe. Everything's soft and warm, and you want to lie down and roll like a kaleidoscope so everything mixes together and your whole body's spinning while you think about the one you love.' Roberta's voice wobbled, but she kept going. 'That's what Erin's feeling. She spends all day and evening trying to ignore it and be the best counsellor in the world for you and me, so I think we can let her have an hour with her boyfriend while we're *asleep*.'

The three girls continued to lie in silence, their backs to her. 'Well?' Roberta asked uncertainly, wiping her eyes. 'Aren't you going to say something?'

'Will you make Nat and Sherry promise not to lie about us?' came a muffled voice. Obviously Roberta wasn't the only one crying.

'I'll talk to them,' Roberta said quickly. 'They were just scared. Honest.'

'They're mean,' said another voice.

'I won't tell on Erin,' said the third.

'You won't?' Quickly Roberta swung the flashlight towards her. Rolling over, the girl blinked in the light. It was Lesley. She shook her head.

'No matter what,' she said. 'I promise.'

'What about you, Patty?' said Roberta, aiming the flashlight at another girl.

'All right,' came her reluctant voice.

'No matter what?' Roberta probed.

'No matter what,' Patty sighed.

'Joanne?' said Roberta, lighting up the third girl.

'I'll think about it,' said Joanne.

Roberta knew she had won. A smile flooded her face and she jumped several times, bouncing light all over the cabin. 'Oh, I love you guys,' she squealed. 'Thank you, thank you. I'll make it up to you, I promise.'

Again the scene faded, leaving Adrien sagged against the side of the cabin. *No matter what,* she thought slowly. Roberta, Sherry, Nat, Cath, Debbie, Lesley, Patty, and Joanne — chance had thrown these eight girls together with Erin Wood twenty years ago, and five of them had died. If the three girls had talked, the five would be alive today, but they had all believed in love. And love was the most precious thing, she realized. It brought the body alive — she could feel it now, just as Roberta had described it, a kaleidoscope that rolled and whispered and hummed in her skin.

There were too many questions without answers — far too many. Suddenly Adrien was so tired, she could hardly hold up her head. Returning to her cabin, she was about to crawl into bed when she encountered two strange pillows. Without another thought, she turned towards Darcie's bed, burrowed into the smell of her own pillow, and fell deeply asleep.

She woke, surrounded by the sleeping of girls, their breathing deep and even, placid as the lake when the air was still. Emerald light streamed through the window above Darcie's bed, shifting with slow leaves. Everything floated on a deep calm.

She was still wearing her clothes and realized she hadn't woken when the others came in last night. In her mind's eye she could see them, tiptoeing down the hall and crawling quietly over the mattresses on the floor so they wouldn't wake her. Gently Adrien drifted with these thoughts, turning and slipping through them like a skinny-dipper. So this was what it felt like when people cared about you, she mused. The air and water, earth and sky belonged to you; there was no difference between walking, swimming or flying; everywhere you went you were home.

Darcie's eyes opened.

'Morning, Spart,' whispered Adrien.

'So you didn't die during the night?' mumbled Darcie.

'Nope,' said Adrien.

'You didn't shit your pants?'

'Nope,' said Adrien.

'Well, that's a relief,' said Darcie. 'Did Connor come in last night?'

'Not that I noticed,' said Adrien.

'I guess that's what matters.' Sitting up, Darcie

stretched. 'I slept all night. I feel like a new woman.'

'Thanks for not waking me up,' said Adrien.

Darcie leaned against the wall and smiled down at her. 'You were hogging the bed, but you looked like an angel sleeping there, so I decided not to bug you.'

The nine-year-old squirt who had lost her ghetto-blaster to Aunt Erin's rules was wearing a red Camp Lakeshore T-shirt. Adrien smiled as she watched the small girl stand in silent adoration next to Aunt Erin, who was dressed in a blue Camp Lakeshore T-shirt. Above their heads the flag rose into the wind, rippling its brilliant red and white, and early-morning voices croaked into 'O Canada', gradually gaining strength. Another day at Camp Lakeshore had begun.

Breakfast was pancakes and bacon. As she stood in the serving line, Adrien was absolutely positive she had never been this hungry. Her first plateful practically dived down her throat, and she joined the line for seconds. When she returned to the table, she found Aunt Erin sitting in her seat, face drawn and tired, talking to Guy.

'Not feeling well,' said her aunt in her usual brusque tone. 'Going to lie down. Maurice is at Ranch Camp for the day. Take over for me, would you?'

'Sure, Erin.' Guy nodded quietly. 'I know the schedule. Don't worry about a thing.'

'I'll handle the office,' Gwen added quickly.

As Aunt Erin stood, she noticed Adrien next to her, holding a plate heaped with pancakes. A faint smile lit her eyes and she placed a hand briefly on her niece's shoulder. Then she walked out.

'You were right,' Gwen said quietly to Guy. 'Lucky you memorized the schedule yesterday.'

'Right about what?' asked Adrien, sitting down.

'First week of camp,' Guy said easily. 'Erin gets over-stressed about mid-week. Then she's over it and the rest of the summer goes fine.'

Adrien didn't buy it. Professional camp staff got stressed out in mid-August, not the third day of July. No longer hungry, she pushed her plate away. 'Is she going to a doctor?' she asked.

'She'll lie down for the day,' said Guy. 'Tomorrow she'll be fine.'

'After one thirty-seven?' muttered Adrien.

Guy gave her a confused look and Adrien decided not to pursue it. 'Never mind,' she said. 'My blood vessels are weak today.' Then she got up to shovel her plateful of food into the garbage.

Paul was early, but still she was waiting outside the office as he coasted to a stop in front of her. Immediately he leaned in for a kiss. Adrien giggled with relief, and they managed several warm sloppy ones before a shrill whistle cut them off. Pulling apart, they saw Guy giving them a ferocious glare.

'Now there'll be none of that while I'm in charge,' he declared. 'No romantic fraternizing, none at all.'

'You're in charge?' Paul grinned. 'Get real.'

'For the day,' Guy said, swaggering. 'And you, scum of

the earth, are helping me put in supports for the Wishing Tree.'

'Aunt Erin's sick,' explained Adrien.

Paul's face went quiet and he disappeared into his thoughts. 'I'll lock my bike,' he said, turning away.

'Would someone please tell me what's going on?' Adrien cried in frustration, looking at Guy. She knew without asking that Paul wouldn't tell her anything, but Guy's face was also closed.

'It's your aunt's business,' he said, heading off to meet the maintenance crew.

By mid-morning the sky had clouded over and a wind had picked up. Children still wanted their Mars Bars and Nibs, but she also sold a few sweatshirts. In her fifteen-minute break she headed to the kitchen. Maybe, she thought, the hairnets would give her some answers.

The kitchen was a frenzy of activity, with aproned figures running from boiling pots to hot ovens to counter tops, all the while maintaining a constant barrage of non-English. 'Excuse me,' Adrien bellowed from the doorway.

The hairnets turned en masse and smiled. 'It's Adrien!' one of them exclaimed. 'The girl who wants to grow up to be a cook.'

'Become a lawyer,' said another. 'Better pay.'

'Better shoes,' said the third. 'Oh, my aching feet.'

A slight pause followed, and Adrien grabbed her chance. 'Could I ask you a question?' she asked.

'Sure, sure,' they chorused and waited.

'What language are you speaking when it's not English?' she asked.

They looked at each other, surprised. 'Ukrainian, dear,' said the nearest one.

'Okay. How d'you say "please" in Ukrainian?'

Now they looked dumbfounded.

'*Proshoo*,' one said quickly.

'No, no, no,' said another. 'Say it slower or she'll never remember. My son forgets every day and I've been telling him for years. *Proshoo*, dear,' she enunciated clearly.

'*Proshoo*,' repeated Adrien.

'She has it!' they exclaimed simultaneously.

Adrien took a long, careful breath. 'Could someone *proshoo* tell me what's going on with my aunt?' she asked.

Instantly the hairnets broke into a volley of Ukrainian, shaking their heads at each other, then turned back to their pots. Resigned, Adrien recognized the signs. There was no point in pushing this one any further.

'Well, could you tell me when Paul Marchand's birthday is, *proshoo*?' she asked loudly.

The smiles came back. 'We've ordered the cake,' said the hairnets. 'Such a nice cake. Sixteen candles. He'll need a big kiss, *proshoo*.'

Adrien flushed but held their eyes determinedly. 'What day, exactly?'

'It's a secret,' they grinned. 'Practise that pucker. Make it good for him.'

It was tough to keep smiling for the seven-year-olds, even Tamai's group. Fortunately no one noticed her mood, even Aunt Erin's nine-year-old fan for life, who came through at ten fifty.

'I see you're wearing a very ugly T-shirt today,' Adrien said, placing the requested Caramilk bar on the counter.

'It's not so bad,' conceded the girl, pulling it out from her chest and assessing it.

'Looks better upside down?' asked Adrien.

The girl flashed her a grin.

'You're doing great with the flag,' Adrien told her.

The girl took the Caramilk bar and stood a moment, smiling at her. 'I like it here,' she said.

'Me too,' said Adrien.

Abruptly Darcie appeared behind the girl, waving something. 'I got mail!' she hollered.

'How come you're not at the range?' asked Adrien.

'It's raining. Haven't you noticed?'

'Just spitting,' said Adrien. 'Robin Hood wouldn't let a few drops of water get him down.'

'Robin Hood didn't have to teach archery to giggling eleven-year-old girls,' scowled Darcie. Coming into the store, she hung around as two more cabins came through, then helped close up for lunch. When Adrien carried the till into the office, her roommate followed at her heels. 'Now, finally,' said Darcie, 'I can show you.' With a flourish, she pulled a stack of photos out of a mail-order envelope. 'Remember that picture I took of you and your aunt last week? I had two copies made. Here's yours.'

Setting down the till, Adrien gave the photograph a

casual glance and her mouth dropped. Darcie had captured the two of them standing on the porch, leaning over the rail and looking down into the camera. Both seemed caught off guard, between expressions, somewhere within themselves. Except for differences in age and hair colour, they could have been the same person.

Darcie laughed and elbowed her. 'You're as gorgeous as she is, Grouch,' she said. 'Didn't you ever notice?'

Gwen got up from her desk and leaned over Adrien's shoulder, nodding without surprise. 'Like mother and daughter, aren't they?'

'Sisters,' said Darcie. 'I'll get another copy made for your aunt.'

'Make it for me,' Adrien said suddenly. 'I'll take her this one.'

Gwen put an arm around her. 'My guess is she'd like it today,' she said quietly.

'That's what I thought,' Adrien said.

Gwen's eyes were thoughtful. 'How about now, Grouch?' she said.

Pausing at the top of the stairs to the master cabin, Adrien pressed her forehead against the screen door and listened to the muffled crying that came from inside. She was about to step into the eye of the storm that whirled around everyone at this camp, she thought slowly, the invisible, mysterious storm no one would acknowledge. Without knocking, she opened the door and entered to find the crying coming from the bedroom, where her aunt lay on the bed, her face shoved into a pillow to keep herself quiet.

'Aunt Erin?' whispered Adrien.

Her aunt lifted a startled face and stared at Adrien as if she didn't recognize her. Her cheeks were blotchy, her eyes swollen. Reaching for a box of Kleenex, she blew her nose, then lay down again, burying her face in the pillow. Carefully Adrien stepped into the silence, walked to the bed, and sat down.

'I brought you something,' she said, placing the photograph next to the pillow. 'Please look.'

Slowly her aunt turned and saw the picture. Picking it up, she held it close to her face. 'That's amazing,' she whispered.

'I like looking like you,' Adrien said.

Her aunt's eyes faltered.

'I like *being* like you,' Adrien added.

Her aunt gave a short, wry laugh. 'True, isn't it? Two peas in a pod.'

'The pod's okay too,' said Adrien.

Her aunt sighed. 'Haven't been a good aunt,' she muttered. 'It's just this week. Things'll get better. Take you out for supper next week, just the two of us.'

'Sure,' said Adrien.

'I'll put this picture on my wall,' her aunt added. 'Next to my desk.'

'Please put the other one away,' Adrien said quietly. 'In a photo album, where it belongs.'

Her aunt breathed in sharply, then pulled the picture of the eight girls from under her pillow and laid it between them. The air pulsed with the unspoken.

'They look like they were very happy,' said Adrien. 'These five.' Gently she touched their faces – Roberta, Nat, Sherry, Cath, Debbie. 'They look happier than most people ever get to be. So do you.'

'Yes,' her aunt said faintly.

Adrien knew she had to respect her aunt's wall of silence. 'Well, I think they loved you very much' she said. 'They wouldn't want you to be unhappy, like you are now.'

Her aunt lay without speaking, looking at the two photographs.

'Neither do I,' added Adrien.

A few tears slid down her aunt's cheek.

'Can I bring you some lunch?' asked Adrien.

'I'm not hungry,' said her aunt.

'Yes, you are,' said Adrien. 'I'm going to get you some lunch right now.'

Quickly she left the cabin, took the outside steps in one jump, and hit the ground running. Minutes later, she returned with a plate piled high with macaroni and coleslaw. 'Drink the milk,' she said, setting a full glass on the night table. 'Good for you.'

Her aunt sat up. 'Never forget a word I say, do you?'

'No,' said Adrien.

Her aunt smiled faintly. 'Have to watch my step.' Reaching for the fork Adrien had brought, she began to eat. 'I *am* hungry,' she said in surprise.

'You eat every single bite,' Adrien said softly. 'I love you, Erin Wood.'

The words hovered between them like insect wings,

flickering in a gold-green down-shaft of light. Then Adrien slipped out of her aunt's startled stare and headed for the cabin's front door, which stood wide open onto the storm clouds building over the lake.

Fourteen

When the whine of a chainsaw tore through the late afternoon, Adrien understood immediately. Ignoring a cabin of eleven-year-old boys who were arguing about the difference between Coke and Pepsi, she climbed over the Tuck-'n'-Tack counter, pushed through their astonished faces, and took off for the Wishing Tree. The rain had let up and she flew through the still-dripping trees unaware of the looks campers were giving her, of Tamai calling her name. As the chainsaw whine cut deeper into her head, it split her brain into a white grinding heat, and the screaming of wood filled her. From every direction she could feel the groan of a great gleaming spirit tilt, lean and begin its fall towards earth. With it went the wishes, the broken-hearted, questing wishes, the whispering hearts of children. Filled with this falling, dizzy with it, Adrien burst into the clearing and spotted Guy bent over a fallen Wishing Tree. Without thinking, she launched herself into the long shock of bodies hitting ground, and then the two of them struggling in the wet grass.

Abruptly the metallic whine cut off, and Adrien saw Paul leaned over them, holding the chainsaw. 'Let her go, Guy,' he said.

'Are you crazy?' yelped Guy. 'She went for me!' Pinning Adrien's arms, he stared down at her. 'She's totally lost her friggin' mind!'

'You're cutting down that tree because Aunt Erin's sick,' Adrien yelled, still fighting. 'She wouldn't let you do it. That tree is sacred. You're killing the wishes of children. You're cutting down their hearts.'

Guy's face changed. 'Grouch,' he said into her face. 'Listen to me, Grouch. Hey, Adrien!'

Adrien stopped struggling.

'We're cutting the *fallen* half,' Guy said dramatically. '*Not* the standing part. We've attached guide ropes, see? Take a look.'

Cautiously she turned her head to see five yellow support ropes running from the standing trunk into the ground.

'Can I let you up now, or are you still going to kill me?' asked Guy. Shamefaced, she nodded and he released her, groaning as he straightened. 'Where'd you learn to tackle?' he muttered. 'The Roughriders? Geez, I wasn't even cutting the damn thing. Why'd you go for me?'

'I saw you first.' Adrien sat up to find her clothing soaked. Her body felt battered from head to toe. Paul gave her a hand and she got to her feet, then stood hugging herself. 'You can't do anything to the fallen part,' she insisted, her teeth chattering. 'It's not dead yet.'

'It will be soon.' Guy reached for the chainsaw.

'No!' Adrien yelled, stepping in front of him. 'Its soul is still in there. You'll murder it.'

'It can wait, Guy,' said Paul.

Guy looked from one of them to the other, shaking his head. 'This has got to be one of the craziest moments of my sweet life,' he muttered. 'All right, put some warning flags around it. You know where they are, Paul?'

'I'll do it right away,' Paul promised.

'I would've done this last week,' Guy said, 'but Erin kept putting me off. She's as crazy as you are.'

Giving Adrien one last incredulous look, he left. Slowly Adrien walked to the tree and knelt by the fallen half. Not much had been removed, a few branches. Placing both hands on the charred bark, she sent her wish deep inside and waited, but there was nothing. And then there was — a delicate tingling that passed from the fallen trunk into her hands, up her arms and into her chest, filling her with a shimmering emerald light.

Without warning the light around her faded and it was night. Above the clearing, a crescent moon held the centre of the sky as five girls dressed in cotton nighties walked through the trees, holding hands and singing. As they approached, Adrien continued kneeling and watched Roberta lead the girls towards her. Sherry was second in line, her long red hair a wild tangle to her waist, then Cath, Debbie and last of all Nat, in an oversized Snoopy T-shirt. Following some unspoken signal, the girls circled the Wishing Tree, Roberta and Nat joined hands, and the five began to sway. Gradually their voices changed, going deep into their throats, the sound muffled, half-buried, as if they had gone down into themselves and were struggling to find something. Then they began to writhe in pain – Adrien could see their hurt as the girls' eyes closed and their faces lifted towards the tree's whispering leaves, sadness pouring from their mouths. Immediately she recognized it: the same sadness she felt within herself, constant, never letting go. Getting to her feet, she stepped into their circle. None of the girls stopped writhing, but room was made for her, and Roberta and Nat took her hands. Adrien's head fell back then and she let her own sadness take her completely; her body swayed and twisted with theirs, her voice a corkscrew of grief. She didn't know why she was crying, only that grief was a song to be sung, part of the beauty of the night, and her body craved it, became more lovely as the song was released. As the girls danced and sang, their music passed into the Wishing Tree and rose along the glow of its bark into the dark, whispering leaves. Then it was over, the girls' sorrow released, their faces shining with joy. Watching the peace on Sherry's face, Adrien wished that just once, this girl's mother could have seen her daughter like this.

'Now we'll make our wishes!' cried Roberta, coming out of the moment of quiet. 'Bums up!'

Giggles bubbled as the girls turned their backs to the tree, flipped up their nighties, and pressed their bare bums to the trunk. Then, amid cries of glee they danced around the clearing, breasts jiggling, arms waving, the tree in a slow dark laugh above them.

The scene dissolved and Adrien returned to a late Wednesday afternoon to find herself standing under the Wishing Tree, the clouds above her opening onto a clear blue sky. Quickly she turned to Paul, her face radiant.

'Adrien,' he whispered, and she wondered what he saw – places opening around her head, angels reaching through?

'Did you see them?' she asked. 'The girls, here around the tree?'

'Just you,' he said. 'You were singing.'

Wanting the warmth of closeness, she reached for him. 'Everything came together,' she said into his neck. 'Happiness and sadness, crying and laughter, the night and the light. Everything touched, and now it's the same heart beating. It used to be war, opposites fighting, but not any more. D'you know what I mean?'

'You were singing the kind of song where you let everything go,' he whispered, pulling her tighter. 'What if it's you? What if you die instead of me?'

'No,' she said, sure of it 'It's not like that. It's not a trade-off. It's each of us, making our own way.'

'Oh God,' Paul moaned, covering his face. 'My birthday's tomorrow and I'm not ready. I don't know enough – when it'll happen or how. If I'm going to die, or if you will. I thought I could figure it out and beat it, but I can't. What'm I supposed to do?'

'It's your birthday,' she said. 'Somehow you'll know.'

'What if I'm wrong?' he whispered.

'You won't be,' said Adrien. 'And I'll be there too – you dreamed it.'

They held tightly to each other.

'Make a wish,' she said. 'Touch the tree and wish.'

'I'm touching you,' said Paul. 'That's my wish.'

He left, not knowing whether to stay or leave, and she stood in the middle of the road, watching the wings that glistened on his back as he rode away. Supper passed in a haze of exhaustion, and then she crawled into Darcie's bed, sleep closing like water over her head. When she next woke it was dark, rain falling steadily outside and the calm, even breathing of girls surrounding her.

Darcie's clock stood at one twenty-two. Heart quickening, Adrien sat up. While she had slept, her clothing had dried and now stuck to her skin. Her shoes were lost somewhere in the corners of the room. Carefully she crept over the sleeping girls, down the hall, and out into the night.

Though it was raining, the moon glimmered through fast-blowing clouds. Reaching the lawn, she began to run, headed for the lake. At the end of the dock she could see a single canoe slipping into the water, carrying five giggling fifteen-year-old girls. Their night held the same rain, but still Adrien could see the girls as clearly as if she was in the overloaded canoe with them: Roberta at the prow, Nat at the stern, Sherry, Cath and Debbie between them.

They were laughing at Nat's lousy steering, but she got the knack quickly and the canoe headed straight towards the deep. Handing her paddle to Cath, Roberta took off her nightie and draped both legs over the prow in an imitation of a mermaid figurehead. Then, without warning, Sherry stood mid-canoe and jumped a cannonball off one side. Crying out, Nat leaned forward to balance the rocking canoe but it tipped, throwing everyone into the water. The heavy frame crashed down on top of the girls, knocking their heads, pulling them under. Quickly the canoe filled with water and sank. Thrashing wildly, three girls surfaced as the first lightning flickered low across the horizon. A storm was building rapidly, kicking up waves around them.

Reaching the ridge, Adrien ran down onto the beach. The girls were crying out, their voices calling to her. How could she reach them? she thought wildly. She couldn't paddle a canoe by herself in a storm.

'Well, if it isn't little Wood,' said a voice.

Startled, Adrien noticed the lone figure sitting beside the dock, and slid to a halt as Connor stood and beckoned. 'Come to make pax?' he asked. 'Come for that canoe ride?'

So, she thought, the midnight camp-fires were a complete bust and the waterfront co-ordinator was out here, sulking in the rain. For a second she hesitated, then stepped onto the dock. Connor was always a reason to walk the other way, but she had to get closer to the girls, see their last moments. If she couldn't bear witness to the very end, everything would be in vain.

She would fail the girls and their spirits, and the reason they had sent her their dreams would be lost. She was part of this, she knew that. But how? And why?

'I was just heading out,' said Connor. In the moonlight, she could see his wet hair plastered to his head.

'In the rain?' asked Adrien.

'I'm an excellent canoeist.' His face remained expressionless and he stood as he had the last time, one hand stretched towards her. Again, lightning flickered across the lake, thunder rumbled, waves rose and crashed. The girls' cries were growing faint. What choice did she have? Adrien thought frantically. She had to hurry. Already, two were gone.

'Okay,' she said and stepped towards Connor.

The night woke up. In the distance there came the slam of the master cabin door and the sound of Aunt Erin's voice calling as she came running across the lawn, yellow jacket flapping.

But Connor hadn't seen the camp director yet. Stepping into a canoe, he said, 'C'mon, Angel.'

'Adrien,' she said automatically, staring out at the lake.

'No!' called her aunt's faraway voice. 'Not her too. You can't have her too.'

Farther out, beyond the drowning girls, Adrien could see the spirits coming awake. Rising half out of the water, their arms reached towards Aunt Erin in a pleading gesture.

'All right,' screamed Aunt Erin as she neared the ridge. 'I let you go. I set you free.'

And the spirits lifted, unfolding from their dreams; as they rose from the water a pair of wings, huge with strength, spread out from each one of them. *Dreaming for two decades*, Adrien thought, staring in wonder. *Aunt Erin's finally let go of them and now they can fly – towards what?*

The loud whine of a dirt bike broke into her consciousness. Turning, she saw Paul riding at full speed through the rain, passing Aunt Erin as he headed straight for the ridge.

Out in the lake, only two girls were still alive, treading water in the storm. As they reached for each other, a bolt of lightning forked gracefully above them, its tiny fingers skipping down to touch the water's surface. Without a sound the girls disappeared beneath the waves and the five spirits lifted free, wings flickering wildly. At the same moment Paul crested the ridge, pulling his bike into a high arc. Instinctively Adrien knew he must have woken from a dream of her and Connor on the dock, and that he had come to save her. The bike's arc was perfect: it would have carried Paul to the edge of the dock where he could have cut Connor off easily, but then a hard shove from behind sent Adrien reeling forward. Helpless, she stumbled directly into the bike's path, forcing Paul to kick free in mid-air, the movement twisting and upending his body. The bike crashed heavily into the water and Paul began to fall headfirst towards the dock.

The spirits were a line of light flowing faster than thought towards the shore. Adrien reached towards them, begging, and the first one entered her, passing through every molecule, travelling every blood vessel, lifting upward into her brain. The next spirit came into her, and the next; she heard each one singing in a clear girl's voice, each spirit *was* voice, the spirits a river of song touching her through and through. The girls had been joy, and so were their spirits. Death hadn't changed this.

Adrien lifted her arms towards Paul, sending the spirits upward into him. One after another they passed through his body, their giant wings outstretched, catching and cradling him, slowing his fall as they sent their pulse of joy deep into the fibres of his being. Leaving him, they flew on towards Aunt Erin, outlining her five times with their wings. Then, beyond Aunt Erin, a place opened in the air, so vivid with leaping colours that Adrien cried out in astonishment. Hands reached from there to here, the five spirits passed through, the place closed itself to human eyes, and was gone.

Above the dock Paul was still falling, slowed by the spirits' passage and his own wings of hope that flickered on his back. Thinking to catch him on her shoulder, Adrien stepped forward. He landed, she stumbled beneath his weight, and there was nothing to catch her as she fell, carrying him, to the dock.

Fifteen

She could feel someone breathing on her lips and opened heavy eyes to see Paul's face hovering just above her own. 'Adrien,' he whispered, but when she tried to lift her hand to touch his mouth, it wouldn't move. To her surprise, she found her arm strapped to her chest. Then she noticed one of Paul's arms was also wrapped in a sling.

'You've been sleeping for hours,' he said. 'We're in the hospital. You dislocated your shoulder and broke your collarbone. I broke two ribs and dislocated my shoulder too, but we're alive. I'm alive, you're alive.'

'Happy birthday,' she grinned. Relief made her giddy, lifted her high above the white hospital room. Paul kissed her nose and she came back down.

'You saved me,' he said quietly. 'I would've landed on my head.'

'Well, I knew you were coming to save me,' said Adrien, trying to joke, but her voice wobbled. 'Besides, I like your head.'

'But with your aneurysm,' said Paul. 'It could've set something off, couldn't it?'

'It was your birthday,' Adrien replied, 'but you still got out of bed to come and rescue me.'

'I woke up around quarter to one and I kept seeing Connor's face,' Paul said tiredly. 'His ugly face, and something about the dock. I didn't like his eyes – nothing there, no feeling. I just knew you were there.'

'The girls were out on the lake,' whispered Adrien, remembering. 'I could see them drowning. Connor said he'd take me for a canoe ride. I thought I could get closer.'

'He shoved you, didn't he?' Paul said angrily. 'I thought I had a clear landing but then you were there, stumbling like you'd been pushed.'

'Yeah,' said Adrien slowly.

'He took off last night,' said Paul. 'Guy told me all his stuff was packed and gone this morning. Must've cleared out while everyone was out there watching the ambulance pick us up.' Abruptly his voice broke and he started kissing her. Closing her eyes, she followed his warm, soft lips across her face, trying to catch them with her mouth.

'Would you look at that!' Guy's cheerful voice declared from the doorway. 'They're both in straitjackets and they're still going at it!'

As Paul straightened, Guy and Aunt Erin entered the room, followed by Adrien's parents.

'Supposed to be in bed, Paul,' Aunt Erin scolded with a smile, but Adrien's father was frowning noticeably and clearing his throat. Then Adrien noticed that Paul wasn't wearing a pyjama top because of his bulky arm support.

That would be more than enough to set her father off, she realized wryly, not to mention the kissing.

'Get you sitting up,' Aunt Erin said quickly, adjusting the bed. 'Guy, take that boy back to his bed.'

Paul gave Adrien one last grin before leaving the room. Then her mother was leaning over her, patting her hair, whispering and kissing her. 'I'm fine, Mom,' Adrien said, but without her old impatience. She would have reached for her mother, but her right arm was strapped to her chest and the left was giving off pains whenever she moved.

'You're lucky,' her father said gruffly, tucking the blankets around her. 'Out running around in the rain. Going out in canoes at night. That boy in here when you should be resting.'

'Shh, Greg. She's not ten any more,' said her mother.

'That boy almost caused the death of her!' exploded Mr Wood.

'No,' protested Adrien. 'He saved me. He knew I was in trouble and he was coming to save me. He has a sixth sense, Dad.'

'Paul's a boy of honour,' Aunt Erin said firmly. 'You need a reference, I'd put my life in his hands.'

Grumbling his way towards a chair, Adrien's father sat down heavily. Her mother and Aunt Erin pulled up two more chairs, and everyone perched on the edge of a nervous silence. With a deep breath, Adrien faced the half-circle of adults around her bed. 'So when can I go back to camp?' she asked. Immediately her parents' faces fell, and she knew she was in for a fight. 'I can still do my job,' she said quickly. 'I only need one hand to work in Tuck-'n'-Tack. Paul's the one out of a job.'

Aunt Erin cracked a thin smile. 'Put him in Tuck-'n'-Tack with you. Be your other hand.'

Adrien burst into a laugh but was silenced by her parents' expressions. Once again, her father cleared his throat. 'You're coming home with us,' he said. 'Doctor McKeown wants to keep you in for observation another day or so, to see if this has affected your brain. Then we'll drive you home.'

'It's just my shoulder, Dad!' Adrien wailed. 'My blood vessels are fine.'

'Doctor's orders,' her father said firmly.

'But I want to go back to camp.' Adrien's tears were sudden and shattering. 'Mom?' she pleaded. 'Please? I'm different there. I like being me when I'm there.'

Her mother swallowed hard, then looked at her sister-in-law. 'Are any of the guest cabins free?'

'Stay with me,' Aunt Erin said immediately. 'You get the bed, I get the couch.'

'And I stay in my cabin?' Adrien pleaded. 'I won't do anything strenuous, I promise. You can even come into Tuck-'n'-Tack and watch me work. I'll sit in your lap.' Blinking rapidly, she watched her father melt. 'Daddy, please? I'm happy there.'

He blinked rapidly back at her, then muttered, 'All that kissing. Very strenuous.'

'We don't kiss much,' Adrien said. 'I just woke up and he was happy I was all right.'

Another loud throat-clearing erupted. 'Yes, I noticed that,' said her father.

How could she convince him she needed to be at camp? Adrien thought frantically. She had to dig deeper into the truth. Maybe he could meet her there.

'I had a dream,' she began, 'just before I woke up. I could see my body. It was dead and the eyes were open. They were blue like they're supposed to be, and they didn't blink or move. There was no breath, no heart-beat. The mouth wasn't smiling, it wasn't crying, it was just ended. I touched the face and it was cold. The skin was sort of grey and hard to move. Like rubber, I guess.'

The three adults breathed as if air was slow, raw pain.

'And then I saw my spirit,' Adrien said, 'floating just above my body. I reached out and touched it. It felt . . . like the sound of a thousand singing bells. Happy bells – the high tinkling ones and the low booming ones. Full of triumph. It felt like laughter.'

Her mother was leaning forward, her mouth open as if she wanted to swallow Adrien's words and take them deep into herself. Their eyes met, completely open doors.

'Mom,' Adrien whispered.

Her mother nodded, then looked at Aunt Erin. 'We'll stay with you, Erin. Thanks for your offer.'

'I dunno,' began her father.

'We'll stay with Erin,' her mother repeated firmly.

Paul was released that evening while she was asleep, but she talked to him on the phone the next morning. Then it was a long wait until Saturday, when the short, round doctor that had been shining lights in her eyes and ordering brain scans agreed to let her out. 'Make sure she takes it easy,' he admonished, 'but happiness is the best medicine. This is a happy camper you've got here.'

The drive back to camp was quiet. As she watched the countryside go by, Adrien floated on a peace that was heavy like dreaming, peace that dreamed like water. When they pulled into the parking lot, it was early evening. The first week of campers had gone home that afternoon and the grounds were quiet. Borrowing a quarter from her mother, she called Paul from the payphone and he said his mother would drive him over to see her in the morning.

'You still dreaming?' she asked suddenly.

'Yeah, I'm dreaming,' he said slowly.

'Not about dying?' she asked.

'It's kind of X-rated these days,' he said. 'Don't tell your dad.'

'I don't tell Dad about those kinds of dreams,' she assured in a rush.

'I hope they're about me,' said Paul.

'Uh-huh,' mumbled Adrien. *Blushing on the phone*, she thought. *How embarrassing.* 'So you have to dream about me too, okay?'

'Uh-huh,' said Paul.

'Promise?'

'Cross my heart, hope to –' He paused, then added, 'Live.'

Kissing her parents goodnight, Adrien let them hold her the way they needed to. Years passed between them then, two years of pain and fear wrapped in love, finally understood. Then she gave her aunt a one-arm hug.

'Hey,' Adrien asked softly. 'Did the spirits say anything to you when they passed through?'

Her aunt let out a quick groan of air. 'Something I've been waiting to hear for a long time.'

'Music?' asked Adrien. 'Singing?'

Her aunt's eyes brimmed with tears. 'They used to sing like that all the time.'

'They still are,' said Adrien. 'Did you know you've got wings on your back?'

'What?' Aunt Erin gave her a confused look.

'Dream wings,' said Adrien. 'They suit you.'

When she reached the cabin, Darcie tucked her into bed, full of advice on how to sleep with a broken collarbone. Except for the two of them, the place was empty. Other staff members were using the free evening to visit family and friends.

'But not me!' declared Darcie. 'Oh no – I had to welcome my best bud back. It's been boring here without you, Grouch. No one complaining, pointing out all my problems, rebelling over the tiniest itsy-bitsy thing.'

'You're a sucker for punishment,' said Adrien. 'Did I ever tell you that I don't like the colour of your nail polish?'

'What's the matter with fuchsia?' asked Darcie.

'It doesn't match Camp Lakeshore T-shirts,' said Adrien.

'Blue, green or red?' Darcie demanded, making a face.

'You should try harder to fit in, Spart,' said Adrien. 'Be a better role model. Don't you realize your nails flash in the sunlight when you're holding a bow? It's very dramatic. The kids'll get all confused if the colours are wrong.'

'Let me see,' said Darcie, rummaging through the bottles of nail polish on the dresser. 'I've got a bottle of forest green.'

'Emerald green?' Adrien asked lazily.

'Nope, none of that,' replied Darcie.

'Forest, then,' said Adrien, falling asleep.

She woke in the earliest part of morning and lay watching the emerald leaves play at the window. The light was calling to her, she understood without words. Standing, she crossed to Darcie's bed and kissed her softly on the cheek.

'That you, Grouch?' Darcie asked sleepily.

'Sweet dreams,' Adrien whispered, and her roommate drifted back to sleep. Leaving the cabin, she walked into the woods, huge with the scent of spruce. All about her the day was beginning, flowers showing their colours, birds opening their beaks with song. Beneath her feet the earth seemed to be humming, restless with its own music. Emerging from the trees, she crossed the lawn, her bare feet leaving tracks in the dew. Ahead, the horizon was vast with pink and amber clouds. Slowly she passed the clearing where the Wishing Tree stood, and an empty Prairie Sky. Then she was at the ridge. Here, she turned to look back at the place that had taught her how much she was loved. For a moment she saw each dear one breathing easy in sleep, and sent a wish into their dreams. Finally she descended the path that led to the beach. A late mayfly settled onto her bare arm and she let it ride as she walked across the cool sand. The lake was quiet, the storm that had been building for twenty years gone now.

She sat on the sand and stared out at the water. Two weeks ago, when she had first arrived with her parents, she had come to the lake immediately, as if called. It had seemed so familiar, as if she had spent the past two years here, dreaming a deep, heavy dream. Now she had come fully awake.

She could feel the wings on her back; they stretched wide to either side, flickering with colours she had never seen – deeper than black, brighter than white. Delicately the mayfly lifted off her arm and flew away. She watched it go, wondering how long she would fly. Two days? Twenty years? But then, wasn't that a question everyone wondered? she thought suddenly. No one knew when death would come, or how. A long, clean breath lifted through her, and Adrien realized she was normal. Maybe the greatest tragedy wasn't how you died, she thought, staring out at the lake, but how you lived your life. So many people lived in full fear of dying. For her, that had changed. She had seen the spirits pass through; when her death came she would know how to follow. The same joy lived on both sides. It would carry her through.

Adrien stood and took two steps towards the great

dreaming water. The gentlest of light touched her brain and she reached with her strong arm, welcoming the horizon.

'I'm alive!' she shouted, and her voice flew across the lake.